the RIVAL

New York Times & *USA Today* Bestselling Author

KENDALL RYAN

About the Book

Dump my cheating ex? *Check.*

Land an amazing job with Boston's professional hockey franchise? *Check.*

Fall stupidly in love with hockey's favorite bad boy? *Ugh.*

After wasting years of my life with the wrong person, I told myself all I wanted was a little no-strings fun. Enter Alex Braun—a wealthy, handsome, notorious playboy who's equal parts charming and dangerous as hell to my wounded heart.

After enduring a very public breakup of his own, the sexy player doesn't want to be anyone's forever. Too bad he barreled his way into my heart, instead of just my bed.

But this professional athlete knows a thing or two about competing, and he won't let go so easily.

Playlist

"Bloodstream" by Stateless

"Help I'm Alive" by Metric

"Lay it All on Me" by Rudimental

"Summertime Sadness" by Lana Del Rey

"Just Say Yes" by Snow Patrol

"Ride" by Cary Brothers

"Hold On To Me" by Placebo

"Running Up That Hill" by Meg Myers

"Lonely" by Sonn & Eyukaliptus

"Careless Love" by Croquet Club

1

ALEX

"**M**orning, Braun. How's the shoulder?" a friendly security guard named Harris asks when I scan my credentials at the door.

I was called into the office today on what's supposed to be my day off, so I'm a little grumpy. But none of that is Harris's fault. I autographed a jersey last season for his little girl. Nice family. I shouldn't take out my annoyance on him this morning, so I fix a polite smile on my face as I enter.

"Getting better every day. Doctor says with a little rest and stretching this summer, it'll be good as new."

"Good deal. Have a great day, Mr. Braun." He smiles and nods as I pass, making my way into the hockey arena where I'm still a new-ish member of the team.

"You too, Harris."

On the elevator ride up to the offices, past the suites and conference rooms, my stomach succeeds in tying itself into an intricate knot. The reason for this impromptu meeting wasn't entirely clear. My agent called this morning saying the Boston Titans' owner had requested a meeting, that I needed to get dressed and drag myself over to the offices.

I have a few ideas what this meeting could be about, and none of them ease my discomfort with the idea of meeting one-on-one with Eden Wynn herself. Because Eden isn't just the team owner, she's also my ex-girlfriend.

Yup, in a weird-as-hell turn of events, my ex is also my boss. Interpret that any way you like.

When I step off the elevator, I'm met with an almost eerie silence. There's not a soul around. Maybe that's the way Eden wants it. *No witnesses.*

Of course, I want to know exactly what I'm walking into, but Eden's pretty assistant, Aspen Ford, isn't here today to announce visitors. Her neat desk sits empty with only a lonely stack of papers. Probably because it's a Sunday, and who the hell in their right mind is here working on a day they're not supposed to be? Eden, that's who.

On one hand, I'm glad Aspen isn't here to distract me. But on the other, I'm oddly disappointed not to see the perky assistant treat me to a shy smile or bite the pad of her thumb while she concentrates on her laptop. Or do a dozen other distracting little things that a normal person probably wouldn't even notice.

I let out a long breath and pause for a second.

The frosted glass door to Eden's office is open, but I knock all the same. I'm as edgy as a naughty student who's been summoned to the principal's office.

Eden looks up from her laptop. "Morning. Come on in."

"Morning," I grumble, entering the office. I stop in front of the desk, and she motions for me to take the seat across from her.

Unease settles over me as I sink into the dark leather club chair. Eden is as poised as ever, her clever eyes not missing my discomfort.

The truth is, I don't like facing off with Eden like this, and *no,* it's not because I still have feelings for her. It's because seeing her reminds me of what a young, stupid kid I was when we were together. Of all the mistakes I made.

After we broke up, it took me a minute to find my groove. And by that, I mean I had a mid-season breakdown and disappeared for six days. Turns out, watching your ex become your boss and fall in love with her new security guard can mess with a guy's head.

But I like to think I've made my way back from the brink. I'm back to playing good hockey again. Not great, but that's what next season is for. I'm primed and ready for a big comeback. First, I just need to deal with whatever it is that *this* is.

Eden studies me for a moment, and I wait for her to speak. I know she won't bring up our past; she's nothing if not a consummate professional. And I'm a fucking vault. No way am I navigating that minefield, especially not today.

"So . . ." I lean back, crossing my arms over my chest. "What's on your mind today, boss?"

She flinches at my cavalier tone before quickly coaxing her expression into a more indifferent one. Her spine straightens and she leans forward, placing her elbows on the desk in front of her. "I want to talk with you about this upcoming season."

I nod. "Figured as much."

The off-season has just begun. I need to get through the next seventy-two hours, and then I'll be heading north to the quiet solitude of Canada for some rest and relaxation at my buddy Saint's fishing cabin.

I've been there before and have fond memories of the place. One of those being the Fourth of July weekend last year when Saint hosted several of the guys for a bachelor weekend. We lit fireworks from the end of the dock. The rookie, Tate, shot a bottle rocket out of his ass crack. I smile inside as I recall the memory.

So, if enduring an excruciating meeting with my ex-slash-boss first is on the agenda, so be it.

"As you know, this game is changing, Alex. The fans are educated and discerning. Gone are the days of the good ol' boys league filled with beer-swigging fans intolerant of anyone or anything that doesn't look and think just like they do."

I nod once, getting it. She's totally right. Things have definitely changed in this business.

The woman seated before me is in large part one of the reasons for that change. Her coming in as a young female owner shook things up, and not in a good way at first. But now my teammate Lundquist has come out as gay and the racial profile of our team has gotten more colorful, both of which are very positive changes. But the fans are ultimately the ones we have to keep happy.

"Get to the point, Eden."

She bristles at my tone. "My point is, there will be certain expectations of our team this year."

I heave out a sigh. "And you're saying . . . you need me to *evolve*." There's a question mark in my words.

At least, I hope that's all she's implying. Because the alternative is that there's no room on the team for a player who spent much of last season nursing hangovers and chasing after puck bunnies. And for the record, I'm not proud of that.

"I need to be able to count on you this year," Eden says, her expression as resolute as her tone.

Uncrossing my arms, I lean forward. "Hockey is my life, Eden. My passion. I'm not going to fuck up this season for us."

She licks her lips, weighing my words. There is no *us*. But Eden's smart enough to know I don't mean us-us. I mean the team-us.

"I know," she says, "but if there's any part of you that wants to be traded . . ."

My eyebrows draw together. "I don't. You think my meltdown was because of—"

"Me. Yes."

"It wasn't," I say insistently.

"Okay." Her voice is softer now.

"You don't believe me?"

"I'm not sure what to believe, Alex."

We exchange sad, uneasy expressions while tension fills the air around us.

When Eden and I first met, I was a bit of a player. I was excelling at college hockey, and between juggling that and a full load of college coursework, I had no plans to be anyone's boyfriend.

But the woman seated before me quickly changed that. One look into her bright, inquisitive eyes made me wonder what it would be like to share more than just one night with her. My curiosity at that turned into a five-year relationship, and then later, a very public breakup.

Back in college, she was a good girl and her attention had been dizzying. I had a lot of female attention, but Eden's felt different. She was brilliant and driven, and her father is the former governor of Massachusetts, for fuck's sake. Her family is like royalty, and yet she only had eyes for me.

That's obviously changed.

"We gonna talk about that rock on your finger?" I tip my chin toward the large diamond that's impossible to miss.

Eden invited me to her upcoming engagement party—well, she invited the whole team, so her engagement wasn't exactly a surprise. But it's still a shock seeing her left finger with a ring on it when once upon a time, I assumed I'd be the one to put it there.

"Did you get our invitation?" she asks, her gaze meeting mine.

I nod. "Yes."

It came in the mail last week, printed on fancy heavyweight cardstock. Seeing her name alongside Holt Rossi's—the brooding outcast from our college days—sent a weird tingle down my spine. Them getting together last season was certainly unexpected.

I wasn't sure I was going to their party. Especially considering the last time I was in the same room with Holt, things came to blows between us. It might be smarter to steer clear of any extracurriculars involving the happy couple. Then again, maybe facing it head-on is just the way to prove I've moved past our breakup.

The party is yet another topic it seems neither

of us is willing to navigate right now as Eden shifts the subject back to hockey.

She folds her hands on the desk in front of her and meets my eyes. "The best thing for you would be to lay low this summer. No drunken bar brawls. No parties. And for God's sake, don't get arrested."

The last time I had a brawl, I was one hundred percent sober. She knows this because the person I was fighting was her fiancé.

Which I guess serves her point.

I understand what she's telling me loud and clear. I can't afford another scandal. It's then that I realize how close to cutting me she's probably been. My stomach twists at the thought. If I don't have hockey, what have I got?

"No parties. No brawls," I say, and I mean it.

"Good. Well, anyway," she says, shifting in the chair like I've made her the slightest bit uncomfortable at bringing up her engagement, and then my subsequent fistfight with the dude. "Thanks for coming in today. I just wanted to meet with you face-to-face and make sure you're certain about this. About being here. I know this must be difficult for you—"

I hold up one hand, stopping her. "It was weird

at first, but I'm fine, Eden. I'm a big boy. I can handle it."

She nods. "I know. Glad we're on the same page."

I rise to my feet. "Well, I guess I'll see you around."

"Enjoy your summer. Just do me one favor." She grins. "Stay out of the tabloid headlines, would you?"

"Don't worry. I plan on it."

2

ASPEN

Sometimes it's easy to pretend everything is fine.

For instance, when I was getting ready for my boss's party tonight, debating comfort versus fashion in the eternal question of shoes, I almost forgot about my heartbreak. Mulling over the hypothetical of *will I dance or won't I*, I was pleasantly distracted. A regular girl again.

But now that I'm waiting outside the club, I feel that dull ache carving away at me again.

What did I expect? Just two weeks after a devastating breakup, and I thought I'd be fine? My first outing since my heart got put through the garbage disposal, and God help me, it's an *engagement* party, no less.

Yep, the Boston Titans' owner, Eden Wynn, and her head of security, Holt Rossi, are engaged. The whole team is here too, swarming around the club entrance like a pack of wolves. Loud, vulgar wolves. But that's hockey players for you—they show you who they are from the get-go.

I pull at my black tunic dress, willing the hem to fall an inch lower on my thighs.

I'm an idiot for agreeing to come. But when you're crashing in your boss's spare room because of said breakup, you kind of owe it to her to go to her party. I couldn't exactly hide out at her house alone. I may be the most amazing executive assistant ever, but I didn't want to lose points for being a lousy friend.

Holt pulls Eden into a side hug, planting a kiss on the crown of her head as their fingers intertwine. They look like a dang cologne commercial, all romance and class. Her in a floor-length, plum-colored gown, him in a well-fitting suit. My heart aches as I watch them, a power couple who are so in love. So comfortable together.

"I hate that PDA shit, Aspen. You know that."

I squeeze my eyes closed, trying to claw my way out of the spiral of bad memories of my ex that threaten to pull me under.

God, this was such a bad idea coming here. I have to keep it together tonight. Having a meltdown in the middle of my boss's very public engagement party would be catastrophic—on so many levels.

"Aspen?"

I blink. Speak of the devil, and she shall appear with a very concerned look on her face.

"Oh, hey. You look amazing," I croak, touching Eden lightly on the arm.

My gaze flits from her to the woman just over her shoulder. *Frick.* Eden's college friend. I forgot her name. *Greta?*

"Are you okay?" Eden tilts her head, and her dark blond waves shimmer under the streetlight.

"Oh, God yes." I choke out the words on a laugh, dragging anxious fingers through my own loose curls. "I just zoned out for a sec. Gretchen, right?" I say to Eden's friend, who has now joined us.

"Yes, Eden and I have been besties since our college days," she says with a smile, the two exchanging a concerned glance that makes a flush creep up my neck.

This must be repeated information. I was probably too busy mud-wrestling the ghost of my ex to hear her the first time.

"Right," I manage to say, smiling back. "I've heard all about you. Do you live in the area?"

From there, it's easy to recover. I'm perfectly capable of small talk, swapping the basics, nodding along when required.

No, I don't mind the weather in Boston. Yes, I've gone to a couple of Red Sox games. I grin and laugh and pretend like every nicety doesn't remind me of how hard I'm faking every second of this evening.

God, this truly sucks.

"I haven't been to a club in ages." Gretchen pouts, her scowl quickly turning coy. "*Someone* decided to get all coupled up, and now a bitch is single with no friends to go dancing with. How about you, Aspen? Any of these fine gentlemen off-limits?"

Gretchen's gaze wanders to the cluster of broad-shouldered hockey players who are chuckling at some inside joke and ignoring us. Which is just as well—one less person I have to make idle chitchat with.

The idea of me dating one of the Titans is so laughably absurd, that my broken little heart nearly lets the comment slide by without so much as skipping a beat.

"No, I—"

"They're ready for us," Holt says, cutting in. He pats the security guy's shoulder before stepping over the threshold, waving for us to follow.

Time to swallow that ever-present lump in my throat, blink back the tears, and smile like I really mean it.

We head inside and the music overwhelms me, thumping in my ears. I follow along down a long hallway and through a door bragging VIP ONLY.

"Gretchen is grabbing drinks. Did you want something? Go catch up with her," Eden says, assuming the natural role of boss in our relationship.

I throw her a dorky salute and turn on my heel toward the crowd gathering around the circular bar. But Gretchen isn't at the counter I squeeze up to. I order a gin and ginger ale anyway—I'm going to need a little buzz to get me through the night.

What do I do now? Head back to Eden and Holt and resign myself to my fate as a third wheel? Try to make friendly conversation with one of the not-so-gentle giants I work with?

I take a sip of my drink, which turns out to be a

lot more gin than ginger ale. Okay, so a lot of buzz to get me through this night.

My phone vibrates. *Thank goodness.* I could use a distraction. It's a text from my mom.

Hey, baby girl. Wondering if you and Dale are coming home for the weekend like we talked about. Let me know.

Okay, not at all the distraction I was looking for. Irrational tears well in my eyes when I see my ex's name.

"Fuck," I whisper, wiping at my wet cheeks with the back of my hand.

I knew I should have told my family right away about our breakup. I freaking *knew* it would bite me in my stupid butt, not getting it over with. Dale's words come back to me.

"I met someone else. We have chemistry. I don't know what else to say. I'm sorry."

My feet move of their own accord, carrying me toward the restrooms, where I squeeze past the line to tuck myself in the corner by the fire escape. I'm kind of an expert at crying in public, and faking a phone call has always been my go-to move.

Angling my body away from any prying eyes,

I tuck my phone against my cheek to hide my somber expression. I have zero intentions of calling my mom back tonight. I just need to look busy while I gulp some much-needed deep breaths and try to compose myself.

"Are you okay?"

I blink open my wet eyes to see that I'm standing in the shadow of a tall figure. "Fine, thanks."

"You sure?"

"U-um, sorry, I'm on a call."

"With who?"

I ignore the persistent stranger, my despair bubbling into a seething rage. *Why can't a girl cry at the club in peace?*

"Seems like an asshole," he says, droning on. "Won't let you get a word in."

I spin around, ready to fend off whatever bullshit flirtation this brainless idiot is trying to pull off, but my words catch in my throat.

My stranger is none other than Alex Braun. Starting center Alex Braun. New team player, Alex Braun. PR menace and my boss's ex-boyfriend, Alex Braun. Don't even get me started on that loaded history.

What the hell is he doing here?

"It's my mom," I manage to say.

"Your mom, huh?"

Ugh. I swipe away one lingering tear from my cheek before I open my mouth again, intending to continue the pretense, but I instantly give up. After all, I'm busted, and I don't even have the energy or desire to make this encounter anything different from what it is.

"Fine, you caught me." I drop the phone in my purse with a huff like the useless prop that it is.

"'Bye, Mom." Alex smirks, leaning against the opposite wall, his wing-tipped shoes brushing my black booties.

He's one of the few men who opted for a slightly more casual look tonight, no suit jacket to hide the corded muscles of his forearms, visible beneath the rolled-up sleeves of his button-down. He tilts his head to the side, his startlingly blue eyes tracing a slow line down my body.

"So, why are you hiding in a corner, Aspen?"

I didn't realize he knew my name. Yes, we've been introduced, but I guess any time a professional athlete actually remembers your name, it's a little jarring.

I take a slow breath, still pulling myself back together. Or at least trying to. "I'm not hiding. I'm recouping."

"Recouping?" He grunts, angling a thick, dark eyebrow. It's like he just *knows*.

"Yo, Alex," a familiar voice calls from down the hall. "I'll be on the balcony."

I catch sight of Price St. James, otherwise known as Saint, one of our defensemen, a bottle of beer in each of his huge hands and an easy smile on his face. He begins climbing the stairs to an upper level where low-slung loveseats and plush chairs await.

I grit my teeth behind a tight, closed-lip smile. Maybe I should keep tabs on the team tonight. At least it would give me something to do other than wallow. I could make sure they don't get too drunk and end up plastered on the tabloid headlines like—

"I'll be there in a sec."

Like Alex. If I were up to that task tonight, he'd be the one I'd be worried about.

Last season was a mess for him with all the drinking, the fighting, the garbage plays . . . the girls he was seen with at clubs just like this one. At one point, Eden believed he was punishing her for their breakup, which seemed likely, given his track record for being . . . well, not a great guy.

Is that why he's here tonight? To punish Eden? Kind of a ballsy move showing up to your ex's engagement party.

"So, where were we?" Alex focuses back on me with a jerk of his chin. "Recouping from what?"

"I'm really fine." I drain the rest of my drink, avoiding direct eye contact.

"Look, I get it." He sighs, waving absently with one hand. "Engagement parties aren't exactly fun. It sucks watching dumbasses in love. Especially when one of them is your ex."

Okay, weird. This is a side of Alex I don't recognize. At. All.

It didn't occur to me that he would be having a hard time too. Maybe he's more three-dimensional than I gave him credit for when he was, well, just a two-dimensional villain in all the tabloids and social media sites. I guess it's kind of heartless to think that I'm love's only casualty.

"Alex, I'm s—"

"Wanna go upstairs with me?"

I blink, my mind flitting back to the terrors of

navigating dirty fraternity houses, where that exact question marked the beginning of the best and worst four years of my life. "Upstairs?"

He lifts a brow. "The balcony. Unless you're looking to get back to the happy couple—or wanting to continue that *phone call* with your mom."

"Oh." I let out a little gasp, shaking my head.

Alex smiles at me then, his lips quirking like he's trying not to laugh at me.

Please don't. Not tonight.

And he doesn't. He just smiles and offers me his elbow. "Let's go."

For some reason, I tuck my hand into the curve of his strong arm, letting him lead me back to the bar. He orders a drink for each of us—another gin and ginger for me, an IPA for him—*and* he even pays. I try not to overthink the gesture, reminding myself that my reaction to his chivalry is because I'm starved for attention these days.

"You remember Aspen," Alex says as we approach.

"Aspen," Saint says in a singsongy way. "Aspen, Aspen. What a name. What's it mean?" he asks, squinting.

Do all the blue-eyed boys flock together just to make me nervous?

"Quaking tree." I settle into the loveseat opposite Saint, while Alex leans against the handrail.

"Aw, Scaredy Sprout." Saint laughs, turning to Alex for affirmation, but the centerman just nods, a frown deepening above his strong, stubbled chin.

"Well, it's pretty. It suits you."

"Thanks," I say, feeling a little delirious. A little outnumbered.

Saint claps his hands. "Ha. That reminds me. Dude, *another* healthy-eating company DM'd me."

Alex shakes his head in disbelief, finally settling into a chair beside mine. "Another?"

"Yeah, they want me to promo some green smoothie on Instagram." Saint fakes a gag for effect.

"Are they local?" I ask, my interest piqued. My voice doesn't sound quite like my own. "You should talk to Eden about it. Maybe she's heard of them."

Saint smirks. "Oh, come on. I always had a hunch you were the *fun* little sister. Don't go dashing my dreams now."

That famous smile miraculously does nothing for me. "I can be fun while still thinking about what's best for the team's image." I glance over at Alex, who averts his gaze.

"Oof, all right, point taken." Saint lifts his palms in surrender, and I smile. "I don't have time to take on another brand sponsorship anyway. I mean, sure, it's money, but I want no obligations this summer other than the ones I'm already committed to, ya feel me?"

"Speaking of the off-season, got any summer plans?" Alex asks, eyeing me as he takes a swig of his beer.

"Looking for a new place to live, mostly," I say. "I can't stay with my boss and her new fiancé forever."

Both men's eyes go wide. *Great.* I momentarily forgot I'm the queen of oversharing to unsuspecting parties.

"Uh, yeah . . . Eden's letting me crash in one of their spare rooms until I get back on my feet."

Alex's expression darkens.

Here it comes . . .

"What's got you off your feet?" he asks, frowning.

I open my mouth to answer, not sure what words will come out. "My ex cheated on me, and we broke up. I lived with him, so when we broke up, I was the one to leave. Which is why I'm crashing with Eden and Holt."

Well. That wasn't so hard, now was it?

Alex's eyes soften, ice melting into warm blue pools. "Shit. I'm sorry."

"It's okay," I lie, adopting my best *I'm fine* smile. "So, if either of you have any leads on affordable places in the area, I'm all ears. Even something temporary, just for the summer."

"Well, how about that." Saint lifts his glass between us in a toast. "Cheers to the broken hearts club."

I chuckle at the idea of Saint being anything *other* than the heartbreaker, but then I realize he's referring to Alex and me. Apparently, we have something in common, after all. "Here's to us."

"You should stay at Saint's cabin for the summer," Alex murmurs as his eyes cut to mine.

I wait for the punch line, but it doesn't come.

"Cabin?" I hear myself asking as the two men exchange a look.

"Saint owns a summer cabin on a lake just outside of Ottawa."

"I didn't know you were from Canada," I say to Saint, who smiles with pride.

"Born and raised."

Makes sense, I suppose. Lots of hockey players are from Canada. And Russia and Sweden.

Alex doesn't relent. "You were saying you needed a caretaker for the place."

Saint tips his head, taking another long drink from his beer. "Yeah. I do."

"And you won't be there this summer?" I fiddle with the straw in my drink.

Saint's expression turns contemplative, his mouth falling into a frown. "I usually make it back every summer, but I don't know if I'll be able to swing it this year. So, yeah, I do need someone there to take care of a few things." He gives Alex a hard look that screams *what the fuck are you up to?*

Staring back at him, Alex says, "Aspen's the boss's executive assistant. Taking care of things is what she does best. Right?"

"Uh, I, um . . . Yes, I guess so."

"She needs a place to live for the summer. You

need someone to stay at the cabin." Alex joins me in the loveseat and leans back, crossing his bulky arms over his broad chest. "It's a win-win."

"How far away is that? Ottawa?"

Wait, am I really considering this? An entire lake house to myself, miles away from my own problems and from Eden and Holt's love-fest? *Heck yes,* I'm considering it.

"It's not quite all the way to Ottawa. It's in a little town in southern Ontario," Alex says. "Six hours by car. Easy drive. Totally doable."

I nod. In six hours, I could get through an audiobook or a few episodes of my favorite podcast. I'd have to stop to pee and eat, but Alex is right— it's totally doable. And I know Eden is fine with me working remotely. Especially in the off-season.

But this all begs the question, how does Alex know so much about Saint's cabin? And why isn't Saint saying much? I direct my gaze toward him.

"It's not that you're not welcome, Aspen," Saint says, staring at Alex. "But as far as the caretaker role is concerned . . ." He scratches his temple.

"Come on, man. She can follow a to-do list."

It's like there's another conversation happening over my head. I swallow nervously, watching their exchange like a riveting game of Ping-Pong.

"The work is . . . manual." Saint says the word cautiously. "Some of it is heavy duty. Clearing brush from the property. Cutting and storing firewood in case I get up there this winter. Changing air filters. Things like that."

"That's why I'll be there to do the heavy lifting. I could go up next weekend and get all that stuff done easily."

Wait, what? My mouth drops open as Alex continues.

"And the pay for the caretaker role is what . . . five thousand dollars?"

"Two." Saint narrows his eyes as he corrects Alex.

"Which is more than generous," I say quickly.

For the first time since all this cabin talk began, both men turn to me.

"So, Aspen." Alex grins at me. "What do you think?"

"Well . . ." I gape for a moment, scrambling for words. "I'm happy to apply for the position if Saint is—"

"It's settled then." Alex smiles with a gentle pat

on my knee that I feel right in my, well *everything*. *Jeez.*

"Congratulations, Scaredy Sprout." Saint chuckles with a bewildered look in his eye. "Looks like you're my new caretaker."

I barely process Saint's firm grip when we shake hands, or what he says before he disappears back downstairs. Something about getting another drink. Oh, and that he'll email me the details.

Right. The details. Of my temporary housing. *What?*

"You're welcome." Alex leans back, his posture casual. Almost cocky.

"I didn't ask you to do that. But . . . thank you."

He shrugs, his gaze dropping from mine to the beer in his hands. "Better than living with Eden and having love shoved in your face, right?"

"Right," I say. Tonight has been . . . a lot. It might be time for me to quit while I'm ahead. "I think it's time for me to call it a night."

"I'll walk you out."

Downstairs, with Alex on my heels, I nearly walk smack into Holt, who deftly lifts his drink over my head and mercifully doesn't spill a drop.

"Sorry."

"You're good." Holt chuckles, offering me a small smile before his eyes narrow on my escort.

"Congratulations on the engagement," Alex says a little stiffly. "It's gonna be a big year."

"Thanks. I know Eden appreciates you coming," Holt says with a polite nod.

A muscle jumps in Alex's jaw, and I can't help but wonder if he still has feelings for our boss.

"I'm going home," I say to Holt. So weird saying *home* when I should really be saying *your fancy place that you're letting me squat in, thank you.* "Send my love to Eden, okay?"

"Will do. You have your key?"

"Yep. 'Bye, Holt."

Outside, the club music is a distant echo. I close my eyes, letting the breeze cool my warm skin. But my ankle buckles when I step into a pothole, my arms flailing wide to regain my balance. Alex catches my wrist before I tumble, steadying me without breaking his stride.

"Thanks," I mutter with a strangled sigh.

I'm really setting quite a reputation for myself tonight, aren't I? The executive assistant who cries in corners and can't be trusted to walk without falling on her face. But Alex doesn't give me any grief, and for that I'm grateful.

"Do you need a ride?" he asks, nodding toward a row of shiny sports cars.

I won't even try to guess which one is his. They all look like they cost ten times my annual salary.

"That's okay. I'll call an Uber," I say, reaching into my purse.

Alex places his hand over mine and thumbs open the app on his phone before handing it to me. "I've got it. Just type in the address."

"Thank you."

"No problem. It's the least I can do."

"No, really," I say, trying again. "Thanks for looking out for me tonight."

He pauses. "It was mutual."

My heart twinges a bit, even as I smile. "Are you gonna be okay?"

He scoffs, running a hand over the dark stubble on his face and glancing back at the club with a cynical expression. "Are you?"

I drop my gaze to the concrete, the familiar

ache settling back in. "I don't know."

Alex steps closer so I'm standing in his shadow again. "Would a hug help?"

I didn't take him for the hugging type, but I find myself nodding all the same. "It couldn't hurt."

His big arms wrap tightly around me as he bows his head and rests his temple against my hair. I surprise myself, bringing my arms around him and clinging.

Relaxing, I release a slow sigh. What is it about the kindness of strangers? But I guess Alex isn't really a stranger anymore. I guess I used to think of him as more of the enemy. The guy who hurt my boss and my friend.

I breathe in against his shirt. I don't know how long we stand there like that, hugging as though we each understand how it feels to be alone, but then I hear the nearing crunch of tires, and I pull back.

"That's my ride." I sigh, lifting my face and bringing one arm between us to return his phone. "Here's your phone, before I f—"

My words are hushed by Alex Braun's full lips pressing against mine and his big hand cradling my cheek. My brain fires off useless information like, *warm, wet, and good. So, so good.* Thoughts that do nothing to clear my confusion.

Instead, I grab a fistful of his shirt, pulling him closer to deepen the kiss, because that's what this is, right? A mind-blowing, entirely forbidden kiss, that's obviously only to make us both forget the heartache.

When the driver honks, Alex chuckles against my mouth, the sound filling me up like a warm cup of coffee. Our lips pull apart with a mutual sigh. I blink up at him, lifting his phone to his chest and pressing it against his pecs—his very well-defined pecs—and over his heart.

"Before I forget," I say belatedly, finishing my sentence breathlessly.

"Thanks." He laughs, low and easy. We're still pressed against each other when he says, "I guess I'll be seeing you."

"In Canada."

"In Canada," he says with a boyish grin.

It's not until I'm tucked into the back seat of an Uber driver's car that reality thunders down.

What the hell did I just get myself into?

3

ALEX

"Oh, look who it is," my sister, Nelle, says excitedly through the phone. "My long-lost little brother."

"I texted you the other day," I say, putting the call on speaker, then sniff a sweatshirt I found in the back of my closet. Deciding it's clean, I shove it into my duffel bag with the other items I'm busy packing.

"Yeah, but that was only because you needed the recipe for my brioche French toast."

"These are facts—but I did contact you." I chuckle, tossing a few pairs of boxer briefs in the bag.

I overhear her say something to Jaxon in the background.

My six-year-old nephew is a handful. Actually, he's a lot like I was as a kid. And considering how I turned out . . . maybe that's not a bad thing? I had a ton of energy, to the point that my parents opted to have me medicated just to get me to focus in school. But once I found hockey, everything seemed to fall into place. Then I had somewhere to direct my energy, and as they say, the rest is history.

"So, the off-season, huh? Are you going to keep your junk in your pants and your ugly mug off the hockey gossip sites this summer?"

"Hello to you too, sis." I roll my eyes.

The sad news is there's a lot of truth to her question. I had a weird season. For the first time since college, I was single, and I might have over-indulged . . . a bit. The media outlets loved to play that up, constantly comparing my lackluster performance on the ice to the prevalence of my extracurricular activities. The two weren't correlated. Last year was challenging for me on a personal level, so it was only natural that some of it spilled over into my professional world.

After my breakup with Eden, my sister started spouting something about my abandonment issues. For obvious reasons, I shut that conversation down quickly.

Do I have issues? Sure, doesn't everybody? But *abandonment*? That made my head hurt—and not in the good, I just ate a whole bunch of ice cream, kind of way. I guess I did feel somewhat let down by my family. But could there be a kernel of truth to Nelle's words about me pushing Eden away because we got too close? Fuck, I don't know.

"Kidding. Kidding. You know I love you," Nelle says when I don't respond, defusing the situation.

My sister is the only person in my family I get along with, so she's allowed to give me shit. The rest of them tend to treat me like a walking ATM. I only hear from my parents when they need something. Same goes for my other relatives. Whether it's them wanting me to invest in some wacky, new business idea, or just to score them tickets to a hockey game—it feels very transactional. I hate that part of being a professional athlete.

That's not to say I don't enjoy being generous. I bought Nelle a minivan after Jaxon was born. Mostly as a joke—before becoming a mom, she swore she'd never drive one. Fun fact? She still drives it.

"I just wanted to call you before I leave the country."

"What?" she all but shrieks out.

I chuckle. "Sorry, that sounded more dramatic than I meant it. Saint offered me his cabin for the summer, so I'm going up to Ottawa to chill for a few days."

When Saint said he needed someone to take care of the cottage this summer, I jumped at the chance. He's from Canada originally, and bought the cabin a few years back, wanting a place where he could enjoy quiet summers during the off-season. This is no rustic log cabin, however. It's a four-thousand-square-foot lodge with five bed-rooms and six bathrooms.

Although now that job is Aspen's, so I debated on going at all.

Sure, I could have hired a local to handle the few tasks Saint was convinced Aspen couldn't manage. But then I decided against it. I need a change of scenery. A break from the day-to-day bullshit that keeps me feeling like I'm underwater.

And the chance to see Aspen again? Let's just say I don't exactly *hate* the idea. She's gorgeous, after all.

Nelle asks a few more questions, but I try to downplay my visit north not only to her, but also to myself.

Ever since I kissed Aspen, I haven't been able to stop thinking about her. And the idea of the two of us being alone together at a cabin in the woods with no one else around for miles . . . it's arousing, to say the least.

"That sounds like a nice getaway," my sister says, snapping me back to reality.

"Yeah, it should be. Saint can't make it up there this summer, so he needs some help with the place—clearing brush and securing the place for winter."

"Cool. Are we still on for New York?"

"Yep, I'll see you then."

I have plans to see my sister in New York in a few weeks. I'll be coaching a youth hockey camp there for a few days, and since Nelle and Jaxon are close enough to visit, I'll meet up with them afterward. I'm sure I'll take them out to lunch and shopping or something. Maybe even play my nephew in some one-on-one. He learned how to skate recently, and I haven't seen his skills in person, only via shaky cell-phone video.

Nelle and I say good-bye, and a few minutes later, I'm opening the front door to let Saint inside.

"Damn. Nice digs, homey," he says, peeking

over my shoulder at the sprawling entryway and sunken formal living room beyond.

We exchange a fist bump.

"Thanks, man. Come on in."

I bought this place a few months ago, but only recently moved in. The house was built in the seventies and needed some major renovations. It was owned by some bigwig finance executive, and apparently he and his wife *really* liked wall-to-wall shag carpeting and gold window treatments. I worked with an architect to take this place down to the studs. Now the rooms are open and bright, and it all suits me much better.

I give Saint the grand tour. We stroll through the cozy family room with its oversize fieldstone fireplace and a view of the pool in the backyard, and the vaulted-ceiling dining room with seating for twelve. I'll probably never even use this table, but the interior designer thought it would fit the room, and it does.

"You gonna host a dinner party or what?" Saint asks, running a palm along the sleek bamboo table.

I shrug. "Maybe a poker night."

"Oh, man. Even better. I'm there."

I show him into the rooms I use most often,

which are my bedroom with its adjoining TV nook where I've fit a small sofa and a huge flatscreen, and the en-suite bathroom. Two huge walk-in closets are beyond that—his and hers. The hers closet is empty, which is totally fine with me for now. I'm not looking to jump into another relationship anytime soon.

We end up inside my bedroom where I have a half-packed duffel bag and some clothes scattered across my bed.

"You still planning on leaving in the morning?" Saint asks, taking a seat on the leather bench at the end of my bed.

"Yeah. It's, what, a seven-hour drive?"

He gives me a sly grin. "Six, jackass. And you know that. You're the one who gave Aspen that factoid. Practically twisted her arm to get her to agree to this."

I become suddenly *very* interested in packing some extra pairs of socks. You can never have too many socks, after all. Then I grab a drawstring bag for my shoes, tucking inside an old pair of sneakers and some work boots, and shove it into the duffel.

"Did she make it okay?" I ask without glancing his way. Aspen had plans to drive up a few days ago, no doubt eager to put her couch-surfing days behind her and to put some distance between her and the city.

Saint makes a noise of agreement. "Cell service is spotty up there, but yeah, she called me when she was pulling into town. I don't assume she had any problems after that."

"Good to hear."

"What's the deal anyway?"

After shoving the socks into my bag, I turn to face him and shrug. "There's no deal."

"Liar." Saint folds his bulky forearms across his chest and waits. He knows I can't stand unfilled silence.

Bastard.

I roll my eyes. "I guess I could relate to the whole shitty breakup thing. Plus, the girl is practically homeless right now. Crashing at Eden and Holt's place?" I shudder at the thought. "I figured she needed the gig more than I did."

He weighs my words, still watching me closely, trying to figure out my angle.

"Dude, I don't have a deal." I hold up both palms. "I swear. Yeah, she's cute as hell. But I'm literally only going to get away for a few days, and to help your ass out."

Saint tosses me the spare key he brought with him. "Helping *me* out? You cost me five grand. *Dick*."

I give him a sharp look. "Yeah, but you can afford it. And I thought you agreed to two?"

He scoffs. "That made me look cheap, so I gave her the five."

I chuckle dryly and tuck the key inside my bag. "Well, remember I'm helping you out *as a friend*. Aspen isn't. She deserves to be paid."

As he shakes his head at me, I hope this game of twenty questions is almost over, because Saint has always had the uncanny ability to see straight through me. And right now, I really don't want him to see how much the thought of being alone with Aspen affects me.

Last weekend, once she agreed to stay at Saint's place, I walked her outside and we waited together on the curb for her ride to arrive. She looked at me like I was some white knight sent to help her. Not fucking likely. I'm not anyone's knight. Yes, I might have helped her by getting her the gig, but trust me, I had very selfish reasons.

Saint's voice interrupts my thoughts. "She's

not a toy for you to play with this summer. You know that, right?"

"Chill, dude. Of course I know that."

He flashes me a conspiratorial grin. "But you *want* to hit that, don't you?"

Isn't that the million-dollar question? Good thing I'm smart enough not to answer.

"All I'm saying is, Aspen Ford is not the kind of girl you fuck around with," Saint says seriously.

I give him an annoyed look. "What the hell's that supposed to mean?"

He straightens his posture. "It means she's the *marrying* kind, bro. So unless you're trying to become someone's *husband*, it means you'd better keep your dick in your pants this summer."

I laugh off his warning, but somewhere deep inside, I wonder if there could be some truth to his words. By all accounts, Aspen is a great catch. But since I'm most definitely *not* looking to be anyone's *anything*, it's all the more reason not to sleep with her.

"In fact, why don't we make this interesting." Saint rubs his hands together as a devious smile forms on his lips.

"What'd you have in mind?"

He grins, crossing his ankles. "If you end up falling for her, you have to get a tattoo on your ass."

A chuckle tumbles from my lips. "Yeah, that's not happening."

The last time I got a tattoo, it was a fucking disaster. I've learned my lesson there.

"Why? You scared I'm going to win? If you keep your word and don't fall in love . . . no tattoo."

I guess he's right, so I shrug. "Fine. If I fall in love, you can pick the damn tattoo yourself."

He laughs, the sound deep and mocking. "Oh, you're on, bro."

After Saint leaves, I finish packing and can't help but reflect on his words. I'm sure he's just trying to give me a hard time—I mean, that bet is ridiculous. Me falling in love? Yeah, that's definitely not happening.

Inside the bathroom, I grab the few items I need off the counter and shove them into a toiletry bag—razor, toothbrush, floss, deodorant . . . all the basics. The box of condoms at the back of the drawer makes me pause.

I swallow a sudden lump in my throat and look

down at the brand-new twelve-pack of size XLs in a black carton that's staring back at me. I debate taking it for half a second before closing the drawer.

Why am I even considering it? I sure as hell don't need a tattoo picked out by Saint. And I sure as hell don't need condoms. I'll only be there for three days, and just like I told Saint, *nothing* is going to happen.

Besides, I've had plenty of fun since my breakup with Eden. Too much, even. Although, is it really called fun if all it does is make you feel even more alone?

Lord knows, I tried. I plastered on a fake smile and went on a couple of dates, hooked up with a few puck bunnies just because they were there and willing, and because I thought it might help. It didn't.

Although, I imagine being with Aspen in that way would be an entirely different experience. She's not a puck bunny looking for one night of fun with a professional hockey player that she can tell all her friends about. She's a good girl. The kind of girl you have to work for. But something tells me it would be worth it.

Still, not happening.

Can you imagine? Sleeping with my ex's assistant? I promised Eden not even two weeks ago that my days of fucking up were behind me. And I meant what I said.

Forgoing the condoms is the right thing to do. Anyway, I'm sure that's *not* what Aspen had in mind when she agreed to this. Yeah, she's achingly beautiful, but like me, she's fresh off a disastrous breakup and needs somewhere to hide out.

Saint was right. I'll just have to keep my hands to myself.

4

ASPEN

I've been at the cabin for three days, and it's official. I'm in love.

In his email, Saint explained that the property is roughly four thousand square feet of magic, and he wasn't exaggerating. It's a cozy haven full of endless possibilities—the Mary Poppins purse of houses. Truth be told, I didn't know what my dream home looked like until now.

The exterior is equal parts rustic and elegant, with a large porch in the front, and a sprawling deck in the back overlooking the kind of view I've only ever seen on screensavers. Inside, the lower level boasts endless windows bragging views of the glittering lake and thick forest from all sides.

The kitchen is modern with a polished wooden island, and a walk-in pantry already stocked with nonperishable essentials. The attached living room is like a warm cocoon with its cherrywood decor, stone fireplace, and a pile of throw blankets, tempting me with promises of long, cozy naps. Upstairs are the bedrooms that have all been collecting dust. A lot of dust.

My caretaker duties will have me working both inside and out. Don't get me wrong, I'm not complaining. What's that saying? "Idle hands are the devil's workshop." I need something to keep my mind off of pretty much everything right now, and this is the perfect distraction.

Saint attached a loose schedule to the email but insisted that I could make my own once I got used to the place. After I inspected the property—checking for dirtiness, wear and tear, the works—I did exactly that and added a few bullet points to the already daunting list. Then I broke the whole schedule down into daily, weekly, and monthly tasks on my Google calendar. Call me anal, call me type A, but I'm not about to do a half-assed job that was given to me more out of generosity than anything else.

Generosity from strange, unexpected places . . .

Which leads me to why I'm currently headfirst in the dirty fireplace, caked in soot up to my elbows, and armed with a broom, a scrub brush, and a bucket of soapy water.

Why start with the fireplace, Aspen? Why not start with one of the easier tasks on the list?

Because I figure if I knock out one of the less pleasant tasks, I'll earn myself some free time later, lying on the deck in my bathing suit and soaking up some vitamin D. Even though there's no one here to know if I'm slacking off, some weird inner part of me still needs to feel I've accomplished something before I indulge in some me-time.

As I scrub, my thoughts once again jump to Alex.

I'd like to think that after working with the Titans organization for over a year now, I've become immune to the allure of hockey players. And the truth is, I am. Basically, anyway. Because while yes, some of the guys are cute and muscular, and yeah, earn startlingly good money, they're just guys who I often see at their worst. Whether it be sweaty, or angry after a game, or when less-than-flattering rumors about rivalries and hookups swirl through the office. And believe me, there have been plenty of rumors about Alex.

So, even if his kindness was unexpected, and the kiss we shared totally out of left field . . . I decided it was a much safer bet to just put it out of my mind.

But knowing that as an objective fact and putting it out of my mind are two very different things. Because while I scrub, I find myself zoning out, daydreaming about the way his thick arms felt wrapped around me. How soft, yet firm, his lips felt against mine . . .

And even if I shouldn't have gotten carried away and kissed him back, it was the first time that night—hell, in a long time—that I wasn't thinking about my stupid ex.

Anyway, I'm sure Alex has already forgotten about it. Or if he hasn't, he's chalked it up to one too many drinks. Or worse, he just felt bad for me. Yep, give the sad girl crying in the back corner a sympathy kiss because nobody else wants her. I can imagine him bragging to Saint, the two of them sharing a good laugh about nailing the boss's executive assistant, yet another conquest to add to the books.

His ex-girlfriend is not only my boss, she's also my friend. And I know Eden would *not* approve of Alex and me even being mentioned in the same sentence.

We may all be employed by the same team, but it's clear that he's the rival. Not someone to associate with. Which is why I'll need to be careful if and when he turns up here. I'm still not even sure if he was serious about helping out with some of the more difficult tasks on Saint's list. But the thought of Alex and me alone out here, with nothing but wilderness for miles around, is distracting.

Channeling my frustration into the scrub brush, I manage to clean away the last of the soot. I cough, slowly extracting myself from the mess to shake the debris from my hair. What a disaster.

Truth is, *I'm* the disaster.

This is my MO and what I always do. I find a guy to latch onto and fantasize about for eternity. That's exactly what I did with Dale, falling hard and fast for him, long before that drunken night together our junior year. I fall in love with the idea of someone before really getting to know them, and then I become so good at making excuses for their bad behavior that I don't even recognize myself anymore.

But I felt like myself with Alex. I didn't try to be anyone I wasn't. I was probably more honest than I should have been about the sad state of my life, and I didn't care for one second what he thought about me. I was just myself.

Sure, it would be easy to dismiss Alex as the

inconsiderate asshole that Eden makes him out to be. But I'm not so sure he's a bad guy. Maybe a little reckless and immature, but not the monster my boss and the media portray him to be. After he found me miserable and practically hiding from the party, he kept me close for the rest of the night, never giving me a hard time or judging me for my Debbie Downer mood. Then he stuck his neck out for me when he didn't need to, and now I have somewhere to live for the summer. And then there was the kiss.

"I guess I'll be seeing you."

The memory of Alex's words sends a trickle of excitement from the back of my neck all the way down my spine. It wasn't a promise, per se, yet I can't help but get my hopes up. Alex Braun and me, alone in a secluded cabin for days on end? The thought curls through my belly, a warm pulse pushing lower and lower . . .

I plunge my hands into the soapy water bucket and rinse the scrub brush. Honestly, my pent-up angst has been useful. The fireplace is already looking much better, and it's taken me half the time I thought it would.

I'm considering which job to tackle next when a car horn beeps, followed by the crunch of tires on loose gravel, and I nearly jump out of my skin.

Oh hell.

I peek out the front window to see that Alex has arrived, pulling in his shiny black Tesla to park next to Ruth, my POS Nissan.

Alex steps out of the car, reaching back in to retrieve a' duffel bag and a box of groceries from the back seat with easy, strong movements. I watch his blue T-shirt ride up a bit as he hikes the bag's strap higher on his shoulder, revealing a sliver of gorgeous tanned skin, and that muscled V-shape that I hear is illegal in most states.

Good thing we're in Canada, eh?

He waves, catching sight of me in the window, and flashes me a devilish smile.

Dear God. How long have I been standing here, drooling over the sight of him? I scramble to pick up what's left of my dignity on the way outside.

"Hey," I call out, momentarily distracted by the sight of his broad shoulders. But when I hold open the front door, my sooty arm re-enters my field of vision, and I cringe. Alex looks hot as hell. Meanwhile, I look like I just stepped out of it. "How was the drive?"

"Easy," he says as he climbs the front steps.

Don't stare at his lips, don't stare at his lips,

don't stare at his—

His mouth curls into an easy smile. "How's it going?"

"Good," I squeak out. "Can I help you carry something?"

As Alex's steely blue eyes assess me, I wonder what he sees when he looks at me. But if he notices that I'm a mess, he doesn't comment on it.

"I've got it."

I step aside to let him in, catching a whiff of his masculine deodorant as he breezes by me. The scent of him—clean laundry and something spicy—seems to fit with the cabin's masculine atmosphere.

"When did you get here?" he calls over his shoulder, heading straight for the kitchen where he begins to empty the box of groceries.

Is that sirloin?

"Tuesday," I say, following him into the kitchen.

"You good? I mean, being here alone. You haven't been . . ."

"Bored?" I shake my head. "No, not at all. There's so much to do here. This place is incredible."

Alex smiles at me again. "That it is."

I watch as he unloads the rest of the groceries he's brought onto the counter. A container of protein powder, a large bunch of bananas, a package of deli meat, and a few other odds and ends. "Are you sure I can't help?"

His thumb skims mine as he hands me a carton of blueberries. "If you like."

My body's response to him is immediate and potent. And probably not normal.

After stashing the blueberries in the fridge, I hesitate, drawing in a deep gulp of oxygen. But Alex doesn't seem to notice as he helps himself to a glass of water from the kitchen sink.

"Well, I should probably go tackle a few more chores from the list."

He lowers the glass of water and meets my eyes. His face is calm, relaxed even, but I'd give anything to know what he's thinking right now. "Eden warned you away from me, didn't she?"

Something inside me flinches. "I didn't tell her you would be here. Honestly, I wasn't even sure if you would come."

"I said I would."

I nod. That was true, he did. But I don't know Alex well enough to know if he's the kind of guy who keeps his promises. I don't have the best history with men who actually do what they say they're going to do. Enter my ex, Dale.

Gathering my courage, I turn to face Alex again. "Why did you invite me here?"

He meets my eyes with an uncertain expression. "You won't like my answer."

"Try me."

He swallows, his Adam's apple bobbing. "You seemed lonely."

Ouch.

Smiling, he leans one hip against the counter. "And I guess I could relate. The two of us at Eden's engagement party . . . I think we were the only people there who looked like we'd taken a puck to the sternum. So, I wanted to help."

I return his kind smile. "Well, you did. You definitely made the night a little less awkward. And I still can't believe I get to spend all summer here, so thank you."

"Trust me, you're doing Saint a favor."

At the mention of his teammate's name, a brief look of uncertainty flashes over Alex's features. But before I can begin to unpack that, it's gone, replaced by that easygoing charm that seems to radiate from him.

"And I'll help you with the bigger items this weekend," he says, "before I head back to Boston."

I nod, trying to ignore the disappointment lodged in my stomach at the thought of him only here for the weekend. "So . . . should we tackle something off the to-do list, or did you want to rest after that drive?"

Alex gives me a playful look, one dark eyebrow quirking. "I was thinking tonight we'd just chill. Besides, you look like you've done enough work for the both of us today."

I laugh, mostly at myself. "Oh, you noticed?" I hold out my blackened arms for inspection.

"Couldn't miss it." He smirks. "Did you fall into an active volcano or something?"

"Ha-ha. For your information, I cleaned the fireplace." I pull at my hair tie, suddenly self-conscious of my soot-filled messy bun. I've never mastered the perfect Instagram-worthy bun.

He smiles and watches me finger-comb my

hair. "You've been working nonstop since you arrived, haven't you?"

"Oh, no. I've been spending some time . . ." I sigh when my hair releases a flurry of ash onto the kitchen floor. "Crap."

Alex chuckles, reaching for the broom. "Don't worry, I've got it. You were saying?"

"This morning I spent a few hours reading on the deck."

I haven't been able to read very much since I began working for the Titans, so I've missed several new releases in my favorite mystery series. It's all about a young femme-fatale detective who solves the crimes of old Hollywood socialites. It's ridiculous and over the top, and I love every word.

"What are you reading?" Alex looks up from the dustpan, his bright eyes knocking the wind right out of me.

I didn't take him for the reading sort. The exploding cars, bikini babes, and killer-shark action-movie sort, but definitely not the *reading* sort.

"A mystery novel," I say quickly, hoping to bypass the part of every conversation where I reveal how much of a freaking nerd I am. "Anyway, I think I'll go wash all this off before I make an even bigger mess."

"Take your time. I'll take care of dinner," Alex says, dumping the contents of the dustpan in the trash.

"Are you sure?" I ask before catching myself, and he gives me a look I'm learning means *did I stutter?* "I mean, you just got here. You probably want to take your bag upstairs and get settled."

"I'm gonna stay in the guesthouse," he says, leaning against the kitchen counter. "I'll head over there later."

"Oh." I gulp. The guesthouse is last on my to-do list. I assumed he'd be staying in the main house with me. "I haven't been out there yet, so I haven't had the chance to make it livable."

"Don't worry about it. A little dust never killed anyone."

I laugh, but it sounds a little too breathy to be natural. Alex graciously ignores or completely misses how much of a weirdo I am.

"Anyway," he says as he glances outside. "It's a nice night, so I thought I'd grill out for us. Are you okay with steak?"

I nod, suddenly deliriously hungry. "That sounds perfect."

"Cool. It'll take about an hour to get everything ready, so you take your time up there."

"Aye-aye, captain." I salute, then turn on my heel and hurry up the stairs before I can process *where the hell* that choice of words came from. Apparently, I turn into a raging nutcase in the company of a handsome hockey player.

It's going to be a very long weekend.

5

ALEX

The pipes creak overhead as Aspen turns on the water. I guess I never thought about how much quieter this place would seem with just the two of us. Last time I was here, there were eight rowdy hockey players taking over every square inch.

I wander around the kitchen, opening and closing cabinets and drawers to reacquaint myself with the layout. Cutlery here, bowls and plates here, wineglasses here . . . I snag two stemless glasses for later.

"Bingo," I mutter under my breath when I find about two dozen bottles of wine neatly tucked away in the pantry.

Picking a red at random, I set it on the island. It's probably an expensive bottle, knowing Saint's tastes, but I also know he won't mind. Then I get to work gathering all the ingredients I need for dinner.

I love cooking, which may be a surprise to some. Unlike playing a competitive sport for a living, I'm in total control in the kitchen, and it feels good. The results are mine and mine alone, and the ingredients do as I say. In hockey, the puck doesn't always go where I want, whether it's a bad shot or blocked by an opponent. What control I lose on the ice, I'm able to take back in the kitchen . . . well, there and in the bedroom, but I can't think about *that* right now, or I'll completely lose focus.

Since I don't trust anything left in the fridge, which are pretty much just old condiments anyway, I whip up a light salad dressing of lemon juice, olive oil, salt, and pepper. It's simple, but it should balance well with the fresh butter lettuce and cucumbers I got from the farmer's stand down the road.

Unfortunately, this won't be my best steak. With more time, I'd have let the meat marinate for a few hours in the fridge. But some oil and seasonings will have to do the trick tonight. Out on the deck, I'm relieved to find that Saint cleaned and covered the grill before he left the cabin last. I turn the dial and the flames click to life.

A book resting on one of the deck chairs catches my eye—Aspen's mystery novel. I walk over and pick it up, skimming the dust jacket.

My focus fades when the woman upstairs fills my thoughts instead. I can't figure out what it is about her that has me so . . . invested. I've always had a thing for blondes, sure. But Aspen is nothing like Eden.

I can't say I ever felt the desire to take care of Eden when we were together; she was always as self-sufficient as they come. I didn't feel the need to wrap her in my arms and *protect* her like I do when Aspen is near me. It's a strange urge, for sure, but it's there all the same, lingering in all our glances and crackling between us like embers in a hearth.

When the meat is cooked through with just a hint of pink inside, I transfer it to a plate to rest before scraping away any residue from the grate. Then I tuck the book under my arm and bring the steaming steaks inside.

At the kitchen island, I find a freshly showered Aspen munching on a piece of cucumber I sliced for salad. Her blond hair is darker now, damp and neatly combed over one shoulder. I've never seen her so comfortable, wearing a slouchy cotton T-shirt and loose shorts that reveal miles of smooth, lightly tanned skin.

"So much for taking your time." I give her a teasing look as I place the steaks on the kitchen island.

She chuckles, her gaze lingering on the wine-glasses sitting side by side that I pulled out earlier. "I'm bad at relaxing."

"Clearly. I figured you needed a break after all your earlier chores."

"Believe me, I took one. That shower in the master bathroom is dreamy," she says, grinning up at me.

Her eyes sparkle with humor, but it's a danger-ous thought to picture Aspen enjoying the massive walk-in shower. Aspen, with her luscious curves dripping wet with soapy water, her cheeks rosy with warmth . . .

My mouth lifts, twitching into a lopsided smirk as I attempt to keep things light between us, since I'm pretty sure the last thing Aspen wants is me picturing her naked.

"That's good to hear." Willing my cock to chill the fuck out, I inhale deeply. "Are you hungry?"

"Starving. And that wine looks nice too."

Smiling, I join her at the island. "I borrowed it from Saint's wine cellar—at the back of the pantry—but I'll replace whatever we take before I go."

"Saint's just the gift that keeps on giving." She smiles sweetly.

I laugh. "Fuck, don't let him hear you call him that."

I grab some silverware and work on plating equal portions of the food for each of us. Then I maneuver the cork from the wine bottle and pour her a hefty glass. When we finally sit down at the table, Aspen squirms with excitement.

"This looks so good," she says, then sighs happily. "Thank you for cooking. I've been living off freezer food for days."

I shrug. "It's no big deal."

"It *is*, though. You can't make a fancy dinner like this and expect me to banish you to the guesthouse." She peers at me over the rim of her wineglass, and my pulse quickens.

"What are you suggesting?"

Maybe it's the alcohol, but a little color blossoms on her cheeks. "Just that you should stay here in the main house. There are a bunch of other bedrooms upstairs to choose from."

Sleeping within mere yards of Aspen? In the

back of my head, I can hear Saint snickering and plotting out which tattoo he has in store for me. "I—"

"No arguing," she says quickly, her eyes focused on mine. "You've done so much for me already, and there's plenty of room for the both of us here. This place is massive. Say you'll stay."

Just say no, Braun. You can do this. Two little letters. N and O. Use them.

"Sure, I'll stay."

Dumbass.

Aspen smiles, wide and bright. It's nearly dark outside, but her sunny disposition lights me up inside. "Good. Cheers."

She raises her glass, and I mirror the movement.

As long as I keep my head on straight, it'll be fine. Why ruin a perfectly good meal by disappointing a beautiful woman?

"Cheers." I savor my first swallow, letting the smooth notes of cherry and tart plum rest on my tongue. I'm no sommelier, but this bottle tastes expensive.

Aspen cuts into her steak. "I hope you don't

mind that I took the master bedroom. In the on-boarding email, Saint insisted that I set up in there, saying it would be 'worth it,' and he was right. That clawfoot tub has become my new best friend. And the king-size bed is out of this world."

"Yeah, he's got some pretty sweet digs." I grunt, mentally batting away thoughts of Aspen naked in the tub, naked in the sheets. *Damn it.* "I've stayed in one of the guest rooms before, so I'll take that room. The master is all yours."

Aspen places the fork between her lips and moans at the bite of steak. "This is amazing."

Shit, that's a sweet sound.

"Good." In my opinion, it's a little overcooked, but if she likes it, I'm happy. If she keeps moaning like that . . . well, *happy* is no excuse for the sudden tightness in my jeans.

"You've been here before, right?" Aspen asks. "You were so familiar with the place when we were talking about it at the club."

"Yeah, we came for Fourth of July weekend last year."

"Oh, that was before I started working for the team. Did E—" She stops abruptly, clearing her throat. "I mean, um . . ."

"Did Eden come too?" I ask, finishing the question for her.

"Yeah," Aspen says a little sheepishly. "Sorry."

"You can say her name, you know."

"I know that. She's my boss and my friend. I just don't want to make you uncomfortable or force you into talking about anything you don't want to talk about. You know, with me."

"I don't mind," I say, finishing my mouthful of steak before talking again. "She's never been here. That one was a guys-only trip. I came one other time for a fishing trip, but by then, Eden and I had already broken up."

Aspen nods. "It must have been nice to come here and get away from the world."

"It was. It's the perfect place to escape from reality."

Normally, talking with someone about the breakup is difficult. They want all the juicy details, the stuff that didn't make the tabloids. But Aspen isn't giving me that impression. Instead, she seems to get it. She's been working with Eden for months now, but she's not picking sides, and I appreciate that more than she'll ever know.

Unexpected questions about my ex teeter on

the tip of my tongue. I've moved on, for sure, but sitting here across from Aspen, it's only natural for the topic to shift to Eden.

"Is . . . is she happy?" My words come out quiet. Stilted.

"You mean with Holt?" Aspen asks softly, and I nod. "Yeah, she's really happy."

"Good," I say, and I mean it.

Breakups suck, of course. But I'm glad Eden is happy. One of us should be after the hell we put each other through.

"So, what about you?" I ask Aspen.

I'm not sure if this is a door I should open, but she's willing to listen to my shit without complaint, so I want to offer that to her as well. The least I can do is ask her about her own troubles.

"What about me?"

"I'm not the only one who had a rough breakup. Although yours is a lot fresher than mine. I guess I just wondered . . ." I pick up my wineglass, hesitating. Maybe this wasn't the best topic to bring up. "You don't have to tell me anything if you don't want to."

Aspen contemplates this for a moment, her

pink lips downturned in a slight frown. "No," she finally murmurs. "I should talk about it. I need to get better at talking about it."

But she doesn't continue. Instead, her mouth seals into a firm line, and she stares at her plate with empty eyes. It would be completely silent if not for the faint chirping of crickets outside.

"What was his name?" I ask, because maybe Aspen needs someone to ask questions instead of navigating this topic on her own.

She blinks up at me, a pained look on her face. "Dale."

I want to make a joke about all the Dales I've known being smelly old dudes at the gym, but this isn't the moment for wiseass comments. "How long were you together?"

"We met at Harvard. He was studying political science, and I was majoring in business. We were together for two years at school, and two years after graduation."

Harvard? Wow. I knew she was smart, but . . . damn.

"What ended things?"

"Oh, it's a long story." She sighs. "I was always really forgiving of him. He had a tough childhood, middle child of four other siblings, parents always on the brink of divorce. He was really depressed in school, didn't have a lot of meaningful friendships. So I kind of became everything to him . . . his friend, his girlfriend, his therapist, his personal bank account. It was exhausting, but I loved him, so that made it worth it."

Aspen has a far-off look in her eye. My chest tightens as I watch her reaction to remembering *Dale the dick* and the hell he obviously put her through. She's a nice girl—Saint was right about that. It pisses me off to know that some guys out there would take advantage of such kindness.

"Then we graduated and began to meet new people out in the 'real world.' I encouraged him to make new friends. And he did, and he seemed really happy and well-adjusted for about a year. But then he told me he had feelings for one of those new friends. At first, he pitched an open relationship, which kind of—um, broke me, but I loved him, so I tried to make it work. I did a ton of research on polyamory and nonconventional relationships, even interviewed some friends of friends. I learned that those kinds of relationships are contingent on trust. The golden rule is to set rules, respect them, lead with love. It seemed doable, but he kept lying. So . . . I ended it."

A heavy silence follows, and I wait for her

to add anything else if she wants to. I personally hope that's the extent of it. From even just the SparkNotes version, it sounds like she's endured enough heartache to last a lifetime.

How do guys like fucking *Dale* get away with hurting girls like Aspen? I clench a fist under the table. I don't even know what the guy looks like, but I want to smash his face through the back of his skull.

When she doesn't continue, I finally speak up. "I'm sorry. He sounds like a piece of shit."

"I should have seen it coming. He refused to talk about the future, and he'd broken up with me twice before. There was a rumor in college that he was cheating on me. The signs were all there. I was just blinded by love, stupidly defending him at every turn."

Wait. Is she seriously blaming herself?

"No, no. None of that is your fault, Aspen. I'll listen to you vent all you want, but none of this self-pity stuff, no *should-haves* or regrets. They're a waste of time, time that you deserve to spend healing. Got it?"

She swallows hard, looking up at me with glassy eyes.

If she cries right now, I'm gonna kick my own ass for bringing this shit up. I'm a fucking idiot. Night one, and I'm making the pretty girl cry. *Fuck, Braun.*

Finally, she nods. "Got it. That kind of talk is for brokenhearted losers anyway. And we are *not* losers."

I grin, leaning over my plate. "Nope. Is this the point where I'm supposed to insert some dumb line about us being birds with broken wings or something?"

Aspen throws her head back with a giggling groan. "Please, no awful poetry attempts. Stay in your lane, Braun."

"Fine." I chuckle, raising my hands in surrender. "I'll stick to what I know. Hockey."

"And cooking," she says, mirroring me by leaning over her plate with a smile.

Damn, she's cute.

"Let's not end dinner on such a sad subject." Aspen scrunches her lips into a pout, tapping one finger on her chin. "Okay, here's my question for you. If you could do anything, *anything* you wanted to, what would it be?"

"Well—"

"Something other than hockey," she says before waving for me to continue.

I pause, a little taken aback. I don't think I've ever been asked this question before. Most of my conversations revolve around the season, getting ready for the season, winning the season, winding down from the season, etc. Lather, rinse, repeat.

People usually assume that hockey is my entire life. Because how dare I have any interests outside of the sport that's made me wealthy and successful?

But the truth is, I think about this topic a lot. I know I won't play hockey forever. And I know there's a lot more to me than who I am on the ice, even if others don't care to see it. Aspen does. So her question and her interest startles me for a second.

I meet her eyes. "I guess it would revolve around cooking. I like making food—for myself, and for others."

"Hmm. Suits you," she says with a knowing smile, swirling the wine in her glass.

"And I'm pretty good at it."

"I'd say you are."

And just because things are starting to feel a

little too date-like, which according to Saint is going to lead to unwanted ass tattoos, I let out a large belch as I rise from the table.

"Gross." Aspen laughs, shaking her head at me.

Smooth, Braun.

It's official. I'm an idiot.

When she stands to clear our plates, I take her hand. "I've got these."

"No way. You cooked. I can clean up." She stacks the plates and carries them to the kitchen.

I follow her. No way she's cleaning up all the mess on her own. I'm a messy cook. The kitchen typically looks like a bomb went off when I'm done.

"My turn to ask a question," I say, rinsing our dishes and stacking them in the dishwasher while Aspen replaces the salt and pepper in their resting place by the stove. "Before, when we were swapping battle scars. Did you drop the h-bomb?"

"The . . . w-what?"

"Harvard."

She chuckles. "*That's* your big question?"

I don't even want to know what my face looks

like right now. "Uh, yeah. It's impressive as hell."

"Yes." She rolls her eyes, but her smile stays fixed between her rosy cheeks. "Does that intimidate you? That I'm smarter than you?" Her mouth twitches.

"Honestly? A little."

Aspen narrows her gaze at me, assessing. "I won't apologize."

"I'd never expect you to."

We grin at each other, the air between us buzzing with the joy of good conversation, delicious food, and great wine. I don't remember the last time I felt this at ease. In fact, I don't know if I've ever—

"All right, Braun," she murmurs, placing one hand briefly on my shoulder before pulling back. "I think it's time for me to turn in for the night."

"What? It's only just past seven." I laugh in disbelief, checking my phone.

Her gaze drifts from mine over to her book, where it sits on the kitchen island. "I like to read before bed. Thanks for bringing my book back in, by the way."

I can't help but wonder if she feels the snapping chemistry between us like I do. Is that the reason she wants to extricate herself from spending more time with me? Maybe she knows drinking a second glass of wine together could lead us into dangerous territory.

Conceding, I sigh. "I'll walk you up."

Once the counters are wiped down, I sling my duffel over my shoulder and lead the way up the stairs. Normally I'm a "ladies first" kind of man. But I'm not about to play that game where I try not to stare at Aspen's ass in those shorts. This time, it's not just out of common decency. It's out of self-preservation.

Just as I'm about to say good night, Aspen pauses at her door, a contemplative look in her eye.

"Why did you stick your neck out for me?" she asks, holding her book tightly against her chest. "Granted, it was super thoughtful of you, but I just want to understand. Why me?"

I lean against the door frame and cross my arms so I don't have to worry about what to do with my hands. "Well, it was gonna be me. Not as a caretaker, per se, but I needed a getaway. I was going to be the one here all summer, doing the chores as a favor for Saint letting me stay here. But then you told me that you were practically homeless and . . .

I don't know. It just clicked. Seemed like the right thing to do."

She blinks at me, her pretty mouth opening and closing as she weighs my words against some inner dispute. Aspen strikes me as the kind of woman who doesn't accept favors easily—from anyone. She's obviously got an independent spirit, and I respect that. But I'm also glad she let me help.

"Thank you," she eventually says with a curious tilt to her head, like she's trying to read me.

I want to point to the book in her arms and say, *You'll have better luck solving that mystery.* Instead, I just stare at the enticing line of her cleavage peeking over the pages.

"That was a weird night, wasn't it?" She laughs a little breathlessly.

The hallway is narrow, and we're standing closer than what's considered appropriate for colleagues. Friends. Whatever it is that we're becoming.

"It definitely turned around," I murmur, my gaze traveling up the line of Aspen's neck to her plush lips, which she wets with a quick dart of her pink tongue.

I remember exactly what her mouth tasted like

. . . ginger ale and lime. I wonder if she tastes like red wine now. My breath hitches in my throat and my heart rate quickens, pumping blood and a flood of desire to my groin.

"For me too." Her voice is low, her pupils wide.

All signs are pointing toward her being interested. And while I know I shouldn't even allow myself to entertain the idea, I can't help but wonder what she'd be like in bed.

I take a step toward her, towering over her petite frame. Close enough that I can feel the warmth of her breath when she sighs.

"One hot kiss aside," she says, her tone casual, "nothing more can happen between us. Okay?"

"You think our kiss was hot?"

She smirks. "Alex, focus."

"Focusing," I say, my voice rough.

"I'm serious." Aspen chews her lower lip. *Damn, that's distracting.* "There's too many people involved."

I nod once. "Understood."

Her gaze lingers on my lips even as she steps into her room. With one last unreadable look, she closes the door softly behind her.

Fucking hell. If my pants were tight before, now they're downright uncomfortable. I scratch the stubble on my cheek that's suddenly itching to get out of my skin.

I retreat into the bedroom across the hall and toss my bag on the bed. There's no way I can possibly go to bed this early. What do I do now? Watch some porn, try to jerk off? That doesn't appeal to me in the slightest.

In the adjoining bathroom, I twist the shower knobs, turning the water on full blast. Then I pull my shirt over my head in one rough movement and kick off my shoes, socks, jeans, and boxer briefs. When I step into the shower and take my dick in my hand, I'm already hard as a rock. No surprise there.

I let the hot spray ease the tense muscles of my shoulders, coaxing me into some semblance of calm as I rub my shaft up and down slowly, until I can't take slow anymore and begin moving my closed fist faster. Shamelessly, I think of Aspen, the soft push and pull of her lips that night we kissed, the moan she made with my meat in her mouth at dinner, the thought of having a rebound fling with my ex's assistant . . .

Fuck.

A wave of pleasure shoots down my spine as I work my cock. I feel the spark closing in on me, the telltale thrust of my hips against my pumping hand.

When I come, hot and thick over my knuckles, it's her name that comes desperately, silently, from my lips. And when I wash the evidence down the drain, it's with an unspoken prayer that this will be the end of it. One hot kiss and a quick jerk-off in the shower, and I'm cured.

But deep down, I know better than that. It'll take a hell of a lot more to cure me of Aspen Ford.

6

ASPEN

After an exceptionally restful night's sleep, I awake to the smell of bacon and cinnamon. Alex must be cooking again, and that makes me smile more than it should.

Last night, I lay in bed thinking about all the things I've been told about him. Arrogant. Selfish. Asshole. Player. Unreliable. But none of them line up with the man I shared dinner with.

He cooked for me. He was thoughtful enough to rescue my book from the deck. And he cleaned up all the dishes, despite my protests that I could handle the kitchen. Plus, he made me smile, and he called my ex a piece of shit for breaking my heart.

I fell asleep with a smile on my lips for the first time in months.

Who would have thought that Alex Braun would be the one to give me a little freaking hope in my life?

I stretch before I get out of bed and make a note to ask Saint what brand of pillows he buys, because these aren't just pillows, they're little clouds of heaven. Then again, I probably couldn't afford them, so I guess I'll just enjoy them while I can.

In the bathroom, I inspect myself in the mirror. I look rested, and I guess I should be. I went to bed awfully early last night because I wasn't quite sure what to do with myself. Hanging out with my boss's ex seemed a little weird, especially after he made me a delicious dinner.

But dinner wasn't weird, so maybe hanging out wouldn't have been weird at all. But it *should* have been. Right?

Briefly, I wonder if I should feel embarrassed about my breakup confession last night. But any idea of embarrassment quickly fades when I remember the kind look in Alex's eyes, the insistence in his voice, and his supportive words of encouragement.

"I'll listen to you vent all you want," he said, his eyes stormy, *"but none of this self-pity stuff, no should-haves or regrets. They're a waste of time,*

time that you deserve to spend healing."

Who knew Alex Braun was so emotionally mature? Hockey god by day, therapist by night. And some part of me needed to hear those words. I just would have never guessed they'd come from Alex, someone I barely know.

I have friends, of course, but I'm not as close to any of them as I probably could be. I don't have that ride-or-die tribe that social media memes like to tell me I should have. Not many people know the real me, but I have a feeling . . . maybe Alex could. It felt so natural opening up to him last night. It was wonderful not having to try to be someone I'm not.

After I brush my teeth and secure my long hair into a messy bun, I follow the smell of breakfast downstairs to a suspiciously empty kitchen. A casserole dish sitting on top of the stove is the source of the cinnamony goodness. The rolls are large and gooey, everything a girl could want in a dessert posing as a breakfast item. Two are missing, which makes me smile. A plate is also on the counter, covered in a cloth napkin. Underneath? Six fat slices of deliciously fried bacon.

Being a late riser doesn't seem half bad. At least, not with Alex around.

I snag a ceramic mug from one of the cabinets

and pour myself a cup of coffee, which he was thoughtful enough to brew as well. I don't bother with the cream or sugar he left out for me. All-nighters at Harvard taught me to respect coffee in its undiluted form. I settle in with my breakfast next to the windows that face the backyard.

My belly flips when I spot Alex outside.

I pause in mid-chew, drinking in the long lines of his body, from his muscled arms bulging under the short sleeves of his white shirt, to the tight stretch of his jeans against his powerful legs. A large ax rests on a chopping block, and he's made an impressive pile of split logs in a nearby wheelbarrow.

There's something about this sexy lumberjack look that has all my attention. Is lumberjack porn a thing? If not, it is now, and I'm thoroughly enjoying it.

His dark hair looks a shade lighter in the golden glow of the morning sun. I admire him for a second longer, but when he pauses to wipe sweat from his forehead, his gaze wanders back toward the house. My heart leaps and I look away, even though I'm pretty sure he can't see me. My own reflection stares back at me with wide, startled eyes.

What am I doing? Ogling a man I have zero

right to? I need to check myself. Alex gave up his summer plans so I could have a place to live—and not even just that. Being here gives me a purpose. A reminder that life doesn't end when a relationship does.

I gulp down my coffee, trying to wash away the guilt lumping up in my throat.

Eden, Holt, Saint, and Alex have all been so generous to me since the breakup. They've provided safety and shelter for me in more ways than one, respecting that I couldn't go back to that black hole of an apartment I leased with His Name Rhymes With Fail. Since arriving here, I've felt so much more like myself. The old me. The before-breakup me. The woman I want to be.

It feels wrong, selfish even, to hog this place all for myself. Once again, I toy with the idea of asking Alex to stay for longer than the weekend. *There's plenty of room for the both of us*, I'd reason with him. *I know I'm not the only one nursing a broken heart.*

I glance back out the window, catching sight of a flash of white against the otherwise green tapestry—Alex's sweat-soaked shirt, clinging to his skin and outlining the muscles of his gorgeous back.

If only he didn't have to leave so soon . . .

Maybe it's for the best. I made myself clear last night, didn't I? One kiss, and no further shenanigans. Behind the heart-to-hearts and lingering glances, danger lies.

Trying to change the course of my thoughts, I remember that the best way to clear my head is to move my body. I finish my breakfast and head back upstairs to change into a pair of heather-blue leggings and a matching sports bra, which feels a little ambitious given my calorie-laden breakfast. But hey, I have no one to impress.

Out on the deck, I unfurl my yoga mat, pop in my earbuds, and scroll through my phone, settling on some meditative music to accompany today's flow. If there was ever a time to relax and unwind, it's now.

I relax into a seated forward fold, immersed in the ambient music. The deck shudders ever so slightly beneath my mat as footsteps near. When I look up, I find Alex resting against the wooden railing, downing a glass of ice water. My heart rate jumps, leaving me lightheaded as my mind tries to catch up.

Our eyes meet, and he gives me a boyish smile. The top of his ears and his cheekbones are flushed, evidence of a long morning in the sun.

I take one last deep breath and pause the music, squinting up at him with a grin. "Good morning, Mr. Lumberjack."

"Good morning, Ms. Yoga Poser." He leans back on his elbows and crosses his feet at the ankle. "Did you eat?"

"Yes, thank you. The bacon was awesome. And cinnamon rolls? I feel so spoiled."

"Good." Alex nods and then tilts his head until we hear a distinct *pop*. He sighs, content. "My mom always made cinnamon rolls the first morning of a vacation. And that's what this is, right?"

"Feels like one, that's for sure," I say, nodding.

"It's definitely one of the happier memories of my childhood."

His statement packs a wallop, and I have a feeling there's a story there. But in the bright morning light, I'm not quite as brave to probe him with questions as I was last night, so I ask what I assume is an easy question.

"Did you guys travel a lot growing up?"

"We camped when I was younger. But then later, everything revolved around hockey, and between the house leagues and the travel league, the family trips stopped."

"I see."

Alex shakes his head, a small smile forming on his lips. "Sorry. I don't know what it is about you, but I feel like I can be open and honest in a way I haven't been with anyone else."

My heart stutters at his admission. "You can. Always. And whatever you share will always stay with me."

"Thank you. I appreciate that."

With nothing further to say, Alex drops his gaze to my yoga mat. "You do that often?"

"Sorta." I shrug. "It's nothing fancy. Mostly stretching. I figure it helps counter how many hours I spend sitting."

"Working?" he asks.

"Yes, and reading." After another beat of silence, I gaze up at him. "While I was sleeping in, it seems you were pretty productive."

He nods, glancing to where I first spotted him. "The firewood is chopped and piled up in the shed where it won't get rained on. Should be enough for the winter."

"That's perfect. You're flying through your list. Saint will be happy."

He shrugs. "Yeah, I guess I am."

As I begin to stand, Alex reaches out one hand, catching mine and pulling me the rest of the way up. Once I'm on two feet, he lets go with no hesitation. No reason to overthink it. But as he continues his thought, I'm still hung up on how big and strong his hand felt around mine.

"I should be done with my share of jobs soon, so I'll probably leave tomorrow morning. Get out of your hair and let you enjoy your summer."

A sudden pang of disappointment flashes through me. "Why don't you stay?" The thought catapults out of my mouth as soon as it's formed. I hear myself say, "There's plenty of room for the both of us here."

Alex doesn't say anything yet. He just watches me. So, of course I keep rambling.

"We won't bother each other, except maybe around meal times. And I know I'd feel a lot more comfortable with someone else here. You know, instead of being alone. This place was supposed to be yours for the summer anyway, and I sort of feel like I messed up your off-season plans."

Yikes. That was a lot to dump on an unsuspecting guy. A little off script, but Alex doesn't seem fazed. He cocks his head to the side and stares at me, and even though we're surrounded on all sides by stunning scenery, all I can see is the blinding blue of his eyes.

"Are you sure?" he finally asks. "That's a big offer."

"Of course I am." I sound a heck of a lot more confident than I am. A gentle breeze reminds me of how exposed my body is, and goose bumps trail down my bare arms and across my stomach.

"Well," he says, scratching at the shadow of dark stubble on his jaw, "if you're cool with it, then so am I."

Relief floods through me. "Good."

I don't know where to take the conversation from here, so instead I scoop up my water bottle and rehydrate. Meanwhile, Alex pulls his shirt up to wipe some sweat from his brow, revealing a full buffet of abs that stir a hunger low in my belly. A dark spot on his left pec catches my eye.

"Nice tattoo." I wipe my wet lips with the back of my hand. From what I can tell, it's a simple black heart. And it's exactly where I pressed his phone that fateful night, just after we kissed.

"Thanks," he mutters, letting his shirt fall back down and rubbing his knuckles against the spot.

"What's it mean?"

"Does it have to mean anything?" His tone is flat and emotionless. I wouldn't say that he was particularly perky before, but there's no question that his mood has taken a downward turn.

"They usually do."

Alex sighs, turning to stare at the trees, his expression blank. "Do you really want to know?"

Clearly, I've stepped on a land mine, and I don't know if I should double down or try to retreat. "I mean, yeah, I'm curious."

"Once upon a time, I got it for Eden. Used to have her initials in it, but after we broke up, I got it filled in. Now it's just . . ." He closes his eyes, letting out a heavy sigh.

"A painful reminder?" I take a small step toward him, tilting my head a bit, as if a different angle will somehow unlock the closed expression on his face.

But when Alex meets my eyes, he just looks . . . tired. "Exactly."

I brush his firm arm with a harmless hook of my right fist. "So, what? Now your heart's closed for business? No room for anyone else to get in there?"

His eyebrow quirks at the swing, and he chews on a smile like he's trying not to laugh. "Something like that. We gotta work on your right hook, Aspen."

"You sure about that? Need to go ice your bruise?"

I wind up for another punch, this time with more intention. But before I can make contact, he twists his body, catching my fist in one hand. This time, his touch lingers.

"Anyway," he murmurs, gently releasing me. "If you're serious about me staying, I only brought enough clothes for the weekend. Unless I do laundry every two days, we should go to town so I can buy more." He pulls at the damp cloth of his shirt, revealing a trail of dark hair that disappears beneath the waistband of his jeans. "It's a forty-five-minute drive, so maybe tomorrow we could make a day of it? Go shopping, then grab lunch at the brewery in town. They make a mean burger."

I blink my eyes away from Alex's masculine physique, focusing back on the conversation at hand. "I'd be down for that."

My twenty-fifth birthday is in two days. I was anticipating spending it alone, cozying up next to the fire with a good book or a movie marathon. But

I could afford to treat myself to something nice, something that will make the occasion special. I have no idea what the shopping scene is like in town, so I guess it'll be a surprise. But at least I'll have good company.

"It's a date then."

7

ALEX

I got in a workout this morning and then emailed my sister back. She'd sent another video of Jaxon learning to skate. I'm probably biased, but the kid is super cute. Now I'm showered and dressed for the day, and am waiting for Aspen to finish getting ready too. Then we're heading into town.

Yesterday was our first full day together, and I'll be honest, it wasn't what I was expecting. First, seeing her in her yoga attire—a figure-hugging pair of leggings and sports bra? It was more than a little distracting. I managed to have a somewhat coherent conversation, but then I needed to go haul wood for another hour just to calm myself down. It was either that, or go manhandle my own wood, and I couldn't exactly sneak away without being obvious.

It's safe to say, Aspen Ford is *not* the woman I thought she was. From my brief interactions with her in her capacity as Eden's assistant, I knew she was organized and intelligent. But I never counted on her being so open, or so easy to be around. And let's not forget funny. Aspen is cool as fuck. She's very likable, and *very* intoxicating.

Maybe it's the fresh Canadian air, but something about being here has allowed us both to drop our walls incredibly fast. I feel like I can truly be myself around a girl for the first time in a long time. It's nice. I'm certainly not trying to impress her or be the guy everyone wants me to be. I'm just *me*.

Well . . . maybe I am trying a little to impress her. Because *hell yeah,* I flexed when she was watching me work yesterday. And so what if my mushroom-swiss omelets were on fucking point this morning? Come on, what guy in his right mind wouldn't want to show off for a woman like Aspen a little?

Last night, I was pleased when she didn't rush off to bed right after dinner like she did the first night. She curled up on the couch and read her book while I looked over a contract for an energy drink company my agent had sent me. We made small talk, and when I discussed the contract a little with her, she gave me her opinion as a friend and not as a colleague.

Today I want to do something nice for Aspen, tomorrow being her birthday and all, even if I haven't known her long. She's alone on her birthday—aside from me, of course—and still mending a broken heart. She deserves to have someone acknowledge it. I guess that someone is going to be me.

I spend fifteen minutes stretching my shoulder with the exercises my physical therapist wanted me to continue with this summer. Thankfully, it feels as good as new.

A few minutes later, Aspen appears, dressed in a pair of denim shorts and an oversize sweatshirt that's falling off one shoulder. I can't help but watch her descend the stairs.

"I hope this isn't too casual. I didn't pack anything fancy."

"Believe me, you'll fit right in. We're not going anywhere fancy."

She smiles and slips her feet into sandals, and I follow her outside, locking the door behind us.

As we climb into my car, she's quiet. Part of me wonders if I said too much yesterday, if I shouldn't have opened up about my tattoo. But Aspen didn't seem to judge me for it, and it's not like any part of my past relationship is some big secret. I have nothing to hide.

I guess I just don't want my past to bite me in the ass, or make Aspen pull back from this easy friendship we've been building. I have a feeling this could be a very good summer, maybe even healing, and I don't want anything stealing that from either of us.

Then again, I could be totally wrong. What I do know is that this is probably the longest amount of time I've spent with a woman without fucking the whole thing up, and I'm not ready for it to end.

"You ready to see the sights?" I ask as I navigate the car toward town.

Aspen rubs her hands together. "Heck yeah. Thanks for suggesting this and taking me with you."

I chuckle at her excitement. "Don't get too excited. You haven't seen the town yet."

She fiddles with the radio until she finds a station that comes in without any static. "What can I expect?"

"Let's see. If memory serves, two stoplights. One main street with a few specialty shops, and a couple of good restaurants."

"That works. A real small-town feel. I'm here

for it," she says, watching the scenery as we pass. There are no other houses, but plenty of large evergreens and a whole lot of blue sky.

"The first time we visited Saint up here, he took all the guys to this pizza place. We couldn't decide if it was the best pizza we'd ever had, or if we were just *really* hungry. But they closed down, so maybe it was the former?"

Aspen chuckles. "Maybe."

"But I'm planning to take you to the brewery, assuming it's still there. I'm not sure if you're into craft brews, but their menu was really extensive too."

"I'm always up for trying new things, so that works for me."

• • •

Over lunch, Aspen and I stuff ourselves with cheeseburgers and the local grapefruit IPA while seated on a great deck overlooking the water. The IPA is just like I remember it, fruity but not sweet. It's delicious.

"Do you have a lot of commitments in the off-season?" she asks, helping herself to one of my fries.

I push my plate closer to her, and she takes another. "Some, not a lot." I fill her in on the kids' hockey camp I'll be helping at in a few weeks, and my planned trip to visit my sister and Jaxon, where hopefully I'll get to skate with him.

Aspen smiles. "Sounds like hockey's your whole life."

"Yeah. For now, anyway." I try not to let this thought depress me. I've always loved the sport, but lately I've been feeling like something's missing. Not wanting to analyze that right now, I turn the conversation back to Aspen. "What about you? What's your story?"

"My story?" She meets my eyes as she takes another sip of her beverage.

"Yeah. Ivy League education. Yoga. Reading. Douchey ex." I wink at her, and she laughs. "What else should I know?"

She shrugs. "I don't know. I guess I'm still working on my story."

"That's fair." It's an idea that resonates with me. Just because you've been known for one thing doesn't mean you don't want something different. Eyeing the plate of fries, I ask, "You want any more of these?"

With a shake of her head, she leans back in her chair. "I'm stuffed."

After lunch, Aspen and I venture into a couple of the stores in town. I stock up on T-shirts, jeans, shorts, and underwear at a shop called Sun and Ski. Then we head into a place that sells gourmet food items like homemade caramels and little jars of honey.

Aspen looks around, inspecting each item carefully, while I buy us a tin of candied pecans. She settles on a box of ginger tea and a little moose ornament, which will be for her Christmas tree, she says. Something to remind her of her summer in Canada.

Next door, we head into an adorable shop where Aspen wants to buy everything. A pumpkin face peel promising smoother skin, an all-natural shampoo for shiny hair, and a balm called Sore Muscle Rescue that she makes a happy noise when she smells. But then she talks herself out of it, insisting she doesn't need any of it.

While she chats with the store owner by the front windows, I sneakily purchase the items and stuff them into a bag.

"One more stop." I point my chin toward the market across the street. "Let's grab some more groceries while we're here."

Aspen nods. "Whatever my personal chef needs."

At this, I chuckle. "Believe me, it's nice cooking for someone other than myself."

"But if you're doing all the cooking, I should at least pay for the groceries."

I shake my head. "Nah, I've got it." I'm all too aware of my salary compared to hers, and there's no way in hell I'm letting her spend her money to feed us.

We pick out a bunch of organic produce and some meat that I can grill for dinner. I sneak in a prepackaged cake mix. I'm no baker, but everyone should have a cake on their birthday, right?

"Anything else?" I ask.

Aspen shakes her head, and I steer our cart toward the checkout lane.

The guy in front of us is focused so intently on the clerk ringing up his groceries, he barely notices his kid, who appears to be about Jaxon's age, tugging on his jeans. The kid finally succeeds with a pleading whisper.

"Dad." He holds up a candy bar he's selected from the stand in the checkout lane. "Can I? Please?"

The man shakes his head. "Not today, bud. Put it back."

The cashier finishes ringing up his order and announces the total.

To be honest, I'm not really paying attention. I'm more interested in covertly checking out Aspen and how good she looks wearing her cut-off jean shorts. But there seems to be an issue, and I look over at the man again, expecting his transaction to be complete.

His face is etched with worry as he counts and then re-counts the bills in his hand. Then he takes a breath and asks how much the bread is.

"It's three thirty-nine, sir," the clerk says quietly.

The man takes the bread off the conveyor belt, and I can see him doing some quick mental math. "And the oranges?"

My chest tightens as I watch the boy's face fall.

"But, Dad . . ."

Acting quickly but stealthily, I take a twenty from my wallet and drop it to the floor. Then I tap the man on the shoulder. He turns to me with a weary expression.

"Excuse me. I think you dropped this?" I bend to the floor to collect the twenty and hold it out to him.

For a moment, there's confusion, but then his expression changes. Gratitude followed by relief.

"Thank you," he says, accepting the twenty-dollar bill and squeezing my hand as I place it in his palm.

I merely nod. "No worries."

The man hands the money to the cashier while the boy watches me with a curious expression.

I consider paying for the candy for the kid too, but decide against it at the last moment because I don't want to interfere with the man's parenting. I merely want to help out in what seems like a desperate situation. Plus, I know from personal experience that my sister would castrate me if I gave Jaxon what she deemed as too much sugar.

Aspen is quiet while we check out. I pay for the groceries, and she helps me gather the bags. When we walk to the car, she bumps her hip into mine.

"That was really nice what you did back there."

"Eh, it was nothing."

She flashes me a skeptical look. "You don't want anyone knowing beneath the tough hockey persona that you're actually a nice guy?"

I grin at her. "Hell no. That would totally ruin my reputation for being a dick."

She chuckles as we load the bags into the car. "Well, I'm on to you."

The warm feeling inside my chest refuses to fade the entire drive back. We listen to music, singing along to an old country station, Aspen laughing at my awful singing voice. She's smiling, though, so I sing even louder. She has a great laugh, and it's easy to make her smile.

Back at the house, we unload our shopping bags onto the dining table.

She unpacks a head of garlic, a package of goat cheese, and a loaf of French bread. "Yum. Look at all this. I can only imagine the kinds of things you'll cook for me."

My grin is immediate. "I have big plans to impress you this summer."

Aspen chuckles. "Confession, I'll be easily impressed. I usually survive on takeout. But as far as I can tell, there's not a single takeout option this far off the beaten path."

"Hey, you do you, girl."

She laughs. "I always do."

Deep down, I do like the idea of impressing her.

• • •

We decide on a light dinner, and I try to teach Aspen how to skewer and grill shrimp.

"That's all you." She grimaces and turns a slight shade of gray at the deveining process, so I take over, pulling the little blue globs from each shrimp.

She's so different from the girls I'm used to. The fact that I'm a professional athlete doesn't seem to faze or impress her, and since she works for the same league that I do, I can just chill.

After we've eaten and cleaned up the kitchen together, Aspen makes us some of the ginger tea she bought today, and I open the candied pecans. Sitting on the couch, we debate topics such as the best action movies, and which are the most impressive goalies in the league. I haven't smiled this much in ages.

"Another confession," Aspen says after a moment of silence. "Dale texted me today."

My stomach tightens at the mention of her douchebag ex. "Oh?"

"Yeah, but I didn't reply. I'm sure it's just going to be some bullshit excuse about how he misses me, and that he's sorry and wants me back. But there's definitely no going back."

I wait for her to continue, but she doesn't. She just takes another sip of her tea, then sets the mug on the coffee table.

She turns to me. "I've decided that I'm in a place where I just want to be single. I want to find me again and be happy with myself. You know what I mean?"

"I know exactly what you mean."

"I mean . . . why date when they make toys that can replace any boyfriend? My life would be so much simpler."

Imagining Aspen using a sex toy is not a visual I can allow myself. I cross my arms over my chest and try to act casual. "Well, just know that if you ever decide to jump back into the dating game, the guy you choose will be a very lucky bastard."

Her breathing slows and her eyes turn molten,

latching onto mine. She gives me a slow blink and then a quick nod. "Thanks, Alex. For everything."

"Of course," I say, my voice coming out rough.

"It's been a big day, so I think it's time for me to go to bed," she says, rising from the couch. "Good night, Alex."

"Sweet dreams, Aspen."

I lock the doors, turn off the lights, and then climb the stairs not long after her.

Despite the comfortable mattress and bazillion-thread-count sheets, I can't seem to get to sleep. My frustration climbs, and I roll over and punch the pillow into place.

Letting out a deep exhale, I know the reason I don't feel tired. Technically speaking, I should be tired. I've worked out *and* done manual labor the past two days, and then spent the day in town, but I'm so fucking worked up that my entire body feels as tight as a wire. And the reason for that is unmistakably my intense attraction to Aspen.

My right hand drifts down beneath the blankets, and I give my semi-erect dick a warning squeeze. Aspen is very pretty, and really fucking cool. But none of that means I need to nail her into next Tuesday.

Jeez. I need to chill.

This trip will be about proving to myself that I can hang out platonically with a female I'm attracted to. It shouldn't be *that* difficult. Maybe it would have been easier to shut down my attraction to Aspen if I'd hooked up with someone more recently. Maybe I wouldn't be this on edge. But honestly, hooking up with a stranger just hasn't appealed to me lately, and it certainly has no appeal to me now.

I suck in a long, slow inhale and scrub my hand over the stubble on my face. I never struggle to get to sleep. Usually, I work so damn hard that the moment my head hits the pillow, I'm out.

It's been a while since I've been this torn up. The last time would have been when I was still in a relationship that I knew wasn't working, when I used to lie in bed at night thinking of my life before the NHL, before Eden. It was easy and fun. I thought being single again was what I needed.

Man, was I wrong.

I miss having someone to lie with in bed at night. Someone to talk to. Someone to laugh and have fun with. I knew it was the right decision to end things with Eden, but I missed the companionship because it wasn't all bad. I loved her, and when we were good, we were really good. But when we were bad, it was the worst.

And now I'm getting to know Aspen, I can see how different things would be with a woman like her. She's so easy to talk to, and it's nice having someone to cook for and spend time with.

Fuck.

I shift on the bed, rolling onto my side. If I have any hope of surviving this summer, I need to find a way to turn off my libido and enjoy this for what it is. A relaxing vacation with absolutely *no* romantic entanglements.

Period. End of story.

If only I believed that, it would make my life a hell of a lot easier.

8

ASPEN

"What do you want to do for your birthday?"

Alex's question shouldn't make me reel the way it does. I look up from my orgasmic breakfast—another specialty of his, sausage-egg-and-cheese wraps. I'm in heaven. Alex stands across the kitchen, drying the sauté pan he's just washed.

"Hello?" he says again, this time with a flicker of humor in his eyes.

"Sorry." I laugh, covering a mouthful with one hand. I finish chewing, mulling over the question. "I don't know. I don't think anyone's ever asked me that, so I'm really not sure how to answer."

Dale certainly never did. After he texted me

yesterday, I made the decision right then to block his number. I don't need his influence affecting my summer plans. Blocking him was easier than I thought it would be, and I wondered why it took me this long to do it.

"Are you serious?" Alex's eyes widen. "Not even Dale the Douche?"

"Yeah, no one. Even him." It's embarrassing to admit that. "I've never done much for my birthday. I'm not one for big parties or anything. And, well, no one has really asked me what I've wanted to do before."

Alex's pity-filled frown softens into a gentle smile. "Unless you want me to round up the locals, it'll just be you and me today."

It'll just be you and me.

I hide my blush behind a laugh. "Honestly, I don't think Saint would want us throwing a rager in his cabin, so I guess you'll do."

Alex rolls his eyes. "I'm honored. So, I'll ask again. What do you want to do?"

Spending the day with Alex is the honest answer. He cooks for me and makes me laugh. But I know he's expecting more, so I say, "Do you, uh, want to go for a hike?"

"Sure," he says without missing a beat. "There are some great trails nearby."

"Not a long one," I say quickly to clarify. "I'm a city girl, and regular exercise isn't something in my routine, so go easy on me."

"All right." He chuckles, his thumbs flying across his phone. After a quick search, he holds up the screen for me to see. "How's this one? Only three miles."

I chew my lip, staring at the map. "I think I could do that."

"Great. Wanna leave in an hour?"

"Sounds good to me."

Coming up with plans with Dale would take so much time and effort. I was always compromising and having to moderate my expectations. Making a plan with Alex, on the other hand, is shockingly easy. Like a business transaction . . . but in a fun and sexy way.

Alex is incredible. Hot, but he doesn't make it his whole identity. Generous, but he doesn't expect anything in return. Exciting, but . . . no, just stop.

You're single and you're going to stay single. There's no way Alex is interested in you, anyway.

I'm not looking for a rebound fling. At all. And definitely not with Alex.

I use the forty minutes or so after breakfast to prepare for an afternoon in the sun. When I'm done, my reflection has me questioning this little adventure altogether.

How do the models in Patagonia catalogs make khaki shorts and long socks look cool and not so . . . geeky? I pull out my high ponytail and redo it lower on my head so my baseball cap rests more comfortably.

Whatever. It's not like I'm trying to impress anybody. Right?

"Nice socks," Alex says as I descend the final step on the staircase.

He, of course, looks amazing. I take him in from head to toe, starting at his black baseball cap, lingering on the straps of his backpack that pull at the tight army-green shirt hugging his pecs, all the way down to his fitted athletic shorts. No long socks to hide those powerful calf muscles.

Who am I kidding? Alex probably *is* a Patagonia model.

"Thanks," I say weakly, leading the way out the front door.

The trail is within walking distance of the cabin, so by the time we reach the first marker, I'm already working up a sweat. The air is thick and humid, like it might rain.

"Did you happen to check the weather before we left?" I ask.

"No." Alex frowns, looking up at the blue sky. He pulls out his phone and huffs at what he finds. "Damn. Rain, but not for two hours. Want to risk it?"

"I have faith in us."

It doesn't start to drizzle until we're already halfway back. Alex is just finishing a story about a family camping trip gone awry when the first droplet splashes against my cheek.

"—poison ivy like you've never seen before. I'm telling you, Nelle just laughed at my misery. And—oh shit, here it comes." Alex reaches out to show me a single drop resting between the manly veins on the back of his hand.

Instinctively, I reach out to wipe it away, and an electric shock zips through my fingers and ignites a warmth between my thighs. When I meet Alex's eyes, he smirks and arches a thick eyebrow.

"Ready to get wet?"

In more ways than one, I almost say as a blush takes over my cheeks, but I can't let that innuendo slide. So I tell him, "It's always a good time to get wet."

The look on his face is worth every word of my reply to him.

Unfortunately, the drizzle turns into a solid rain in minutes. Soon, we're laughing as it begins to pour, the raindrops turning our clothes a shade darker.

"How far are we from the cabin?" I ask, squinting through the downpour.

"About twenty minutes, give or take."

"I'm not much of a runner, so if you want to go ahead, I can meet you back there."

Alex scoffs. "I'm not leaving you."

My heart does a happy little pirouette in my chest, and I hide my smile beneath the bill of my cap.

We walk until we're soaked to the bone by the summer rain. The sun peeks out from behind the clouds, casting fragmented rainbows across the sky, but the rain's just getting started, based on the darkening clouds moving our way.

When we make it back to the cabin, we linger on the porch to kick off our shoes and wring out our clothes—at least, whatever we can manage without taking them off completely. When Alex lifts his shirt to shake some of the rain from it, my gaze snags on his oblique muscles that dip into the low waistband of his shorts. I'm mesmerized.

"How about we change, and then I'll get started on lunch," Alex says with a friendly grin, his tone teasing.

Crap. He definitely caught me staring.

"Cool," I choke out, leading the way indoors.

Once I've peeled off my wet clothes and towel-dried my hair, I find myself wishing I'd packed more than shorts and yoga pants. Maybe a sundress would have been nice. But then again, I'm not here to impress anyone, and Alex wasn't intending to stay all summer.

Not that I want to impress him or anything.

I settle on some cozy, and most importantly, dry clothes—a gray knit sweater, drawstring shorts, and matching chunky socks.

By the time I wander into the kitchen, Alex is already changed, busy at the island assembling two sandwiches.

"What's next on the docket?" he asks, handing me a plate holding a turkey and cheddar sandwich.

Be still my heart. The man even put lettuce and tomato on it.

"I don't know," I say between perfectly delicious bites. "Nothing outdoors, I suppose."

The rain is coming down harder now, and the sky has turned an ominous shade of gray.

"That makes sense," Alex says. "But it's still your birthday. I'm game for whatever."

Since he's facing away from me, I let myself stare at the curve of his broad, muscular shoulders, and appreciate the messiness of his still-damp hair.

"I'll try to think of something," I say.

Alex squeezes my shoulder as he passes me to clean up the kitchen.

When I finish my last bite, the kitchen is sparkling clean again, and Alex has taken his phone and made himself scarce.

I can hear him speaking to someone in a hushed tone, and curiosity spirals through me. Could it be a woman? If so, he hasn't mentioned anyone special. Curious, I wander into the living room a few minutes later and find he's stacked board games and puzzles on the coffee table.

"This is the best I could come up with," he says, appearing behind me. "Sorry about the rain."

I wave him off. "It's not your fault. And I don't mind the rain."

Alex shoves one hand in his pocket. "Still, it probably makes for a lame birthday."

I inspect an old-fashioned game of Clue and shake my head. "When I accepted this gig, I figured I'd be spending my birthday by myself. Believe me when I tell you that this is better than being alone."

He nods in agreement. "Good. And just so you know, I'm up for anything."

I raise one brow. "Anything?"

Alex chuckles. "Skinny-dipping in the lake . . . streaking through the rain . . . drinking games that involve clothes being removed. You name it."

"You are dangerous." I shake my head, grinning at him. "Would it be totally lame if I wanted to take a bubble bath?"

"Not lame at all." His eyes meet mine, what appears to be heat building in them as he looks at me. "Especially if you let me pour you a glass of the champagne I have chilling in the fridge."

My heart flutters at this unexpected sweetness. "A glass of champagne would be perfect."

I grab my book, but don't end up reading it. Alex delivers the glass of champagne to my room while I'm filling the tub.

"Thanks," I murmur, my fingers brushing his as I accept the glass.

I close the door and am about to get into the tub when there's a sudden knock at the door.

"Just a second," I call out. Wrapping myself in a towel, I open the door.

Alex is holding a shopping bag, and I recognize the logo from the organic skincare shop we ventured into in town.

"What's this?" I ask when he holds it out to me.

"Just some things for your birthday. It's nothing big, but I saw you admiring them in the store, and wanted to get them for you."

My brow scrunches as I peek inside. The pumpkin face peel and body wash, shampoo with essential oils, bubble bath . . . all the items I'd looked at and put back because I didn't need them, and couldn't afford them anyway.

"Y-you got this for me?"

Smiling, Alex nods. "Happy birthday, Aspen."

"Thank you." I consider hugging him, but since I'm naked beneath the towel, decide I'd better not. "That was very thoughtful of you."

His mouth lifts in a smile. "Enjoy. You deserve to relax on your birthday."

Suddenly speechless, I give him a little nod.

The whole scene is so comfortable and domestic between the two of us, and the rain pattering against the roof and windows makes everything feel a little dreamy. I find it hard to focus with him nearby. And when I step into the tub and lower myself into the warm water, he's not far from my thoughts.

It's safe to say this is *not* the guy Eden led me to believe Alex was and who she warned me about. Where is the hot-tempered jerk? The man who left her and crushed her heart?

I need to rewrite everything I've heard about Alex, and I'm okay with that. I'm going in with my eyes wide open and making my own decisions from here on out.

Once I'm thoroughly washed, scrubbed, and relaxed, I shuffle back into the kitchen. I peek over his shoulder to see what he's making. "Is that for dinner?"

"Yep," he says. So far, he's sliced up some lemons, onions, garlic, and parsley into neat piles.

"What can I do?"

"You can pour yourself a glass of wine and pick a movie for after dinner."

I roll my eyes with a dumb grin plastered on my face. "*Fine*," I say dramatically, like what he's asked me to do is some hardship. "*Any* movie?"

"Any movie."

With an evil little laugh, I clap my hands, then head back to the living room with an excited skip in my step. I locate a romantic comedy on Netflix, just as Alex calls me back into the kitchen for dinner.

My heart skips a beat at the sight of the table—candles, two chilled glasses of white wine, and the food? Straight out of Instagram. A lightly breaded chicken breast rests on each plate in a bed of buttery angel hair pasta, generously adorned with lemon halves and fresh parsley. I gaze at Alex with a bewildered look.

"Chicken piccata," he says, sensing my question. "It's a twist on an old family recipe."

"Are you secretly from an elite line of master chefs?"

I giggle, sinking into my seat. He joins me, and I notice his hair has dried into a messy style that looks perfectly rumpled.

"Not that I know of. It's a favorite of mine, especially on rainy days. Not too heavy, but definitely counts as comfort food."

"My comfort food usually comes in a Styrofoam container."

"Not on your birthday."

We dig in. The food is *so* good, and the company? Let's just say I'm definitely going to remember this birthday as one of the best I've ever had. Soon, we're leaning back in our chairs, full and content.

"There's a cake cooling on the counter," Alex says over the rim of his wineglass. "Do you want a slice now, or should we wait until after we start the movie?"

"You baked a cake?" I ask, my eyes wide.

"You can't celebrate your birthday without having cake."

This man . . . blowing every single expectation out of the water. I don't know if I have enough room for cake, but I'm so blissed out that all I can do is smile and nod like an idiot.

Alex reluctantly agrees to let me help clean up, so I rinse the dishes and load them into the dishwasher. Our elbows brush as he slices the cake, which is dark chocolate and smells delicious.

"Shit. I forgot frosting. I feel like an idiot," he says, shaking his head.

"Oh my gosh, don't. Alex, I love this so much. It's another thing I don't usually get on my birthday, so thank you."

"I'll say this up front—I'm a cook, *not* a baker," he grumbles when he presents the finished product. It's an adorably lopsided slice of cake, with a single birthday candle sitting at a laughable angle. "Make a wish."

I smirk and lean in toward the candle. "Oh, you aren't going to sing for me?"

"You really want me to?"

I pretend to mull it over. "Nah, I think I've heard enough of your singing."

Alex's low rumble of laughter coils deep in my belly. I lean in further and blow out the candle.

"What did you wish for?"

"I can't tell you or it won't come true." I wink.

The couch feels smaller now with the two of us curled into opposite sides. Turns out, I definitely have room for cake, sighing as each moist mouthful brings me more pleasure than sex with my ex ever did. In my peripheral vision, Alex is watching me, an unreadable expression on his face.

When the movie starts, I lift my wineglass. "Cheers."

He smiles at me. "Happy birthday."

We watch the opening scenes together in comfortable silence. Until Alex scoffs.

"This is so unrealistic." He crosses his arms over his chest and shakes his head. The two leads in the movie have just agreed to pretend to be married in order to fool the hero's grandfather into releasing his inheritance.

"That's kind of the point." I laugh, poking his thigh with my toe.

My cheeks are already warm with wine, so it's super easy to decide to leave my foot pressed against the hard muscle of his leg. He wraps one of those big strong hands around my sock, just over my ankle, and I nearly lose all feeling in my lower body.

Does Alex have any idea what he's doing to me?

The rest of the film passes by in a blur of laughter and far too much wine. When the credits finally roll, his hand is still resting on me. The wine has made me bolder, so I turn my body, stretching both legs over his lap with an exaggerated yawn. His hands find my feet again, this time massaging them with deliberate strokes. A shiver ripples up my legs and into my core.

"Mmm." I tilt my head back with a moan. "My feet are sore from the hike."

"I thought they might be," Alex murmurs, his voice dark.

When he finds a particularly tender spot and digs in, I muffle a groan against the back of my hand. And that unreadable expression I keep trying to decipher that washes over his face? Maybe it's the wine, but it's looking more and more like desire. Desire for *me*.

I prop my head on my elbow and watch him unabashedly. The massage is long over by the time one of us speaks again.

"What now?" he asks, wetting his lips with a quick swipe of his tongue.

"We should go to bed," I say softly.

It's only been a few days since our first night at the cabin, and I'm already regretting the line I drew between us. Maybe rebound sex is what both of us need? Well, what *I* need.

I stand, and the room spins only a tiny bit. Alex steadies me with strong hands on my waist, and I lean into his solid body.

"Let's get you up those stairs."

I'm not nearly as drunk as he thinks I am, but I still let Alex guide me up the stairs. I like the feel of his big hands pressed against me, the way his fingers squeeze around my hips when I stumble.

What would his hands feel like on my bare skin?

At the door to my room, I take his hand and slide my thumbs over his knuckles. "Thank you for the best birthday."

His crooked smile is flirtatious. "The best?"

I close my eyes and nod solemnly, wrapping my arms around him. Sighing, I press my cheek against his pec, and he returns the hug. He smells like rain and chocolate cake, an intoxicating duo.

If I lean back, I wonder if he'll . . .

But Alex releases me from the hug with a short

"good night," and before I can even blink, he's turned and heading toward his door. Disappointment folds inside me like a wilting flower, and I turn and shuffle into my own room, flopping onto my bed with a huff.

What was I expecting? Me, the office's honorary nerd, hooking up with hockey's number one bad boy? Yeah, not likely.

I don't know the first thing about one-night stands. I was with Dale since I was twenty, just barely out of adolescence. I never learned the ins and outs of a casual hookup.

It seems simple enough. Attraction plus lust times flirting and *bam*, the interested parties fall in bed together. If anyone's the poster boy for casual sex, it's Alex Braun. The guy is funny and sweet, all wrapped up in one hotter-than-hell package. I could spend the rest of this summer fantasizing about him, but I'll never be brave enough to tell him what I want.

Chewing on my lip, I stare at the ceiling. Maybe there's another way . . . one where I don't have to say it outright. They do say that actions speak louder than words. All I have to do is walk into his bedroom and crawl in bed with him, and just *take* what I want . . . assuming he wants the same thing.

My heart pounds in my chest, and my cheeks burn hot.

Who the heck am I kidding? I'm no temptress. I'd probably just make a fool of myself and end up sulking back here, embarrassed and defeated.

I scrunch my eyes closed, but I can't shake the thought. It could be so easy. So . . . game-changing. It is my birthday, after all.

And aren't you supposed to do what you want on your birthday? And what I want to *do* is Alex.

9

ALEX

Man, tonight was a roller coaster—equal parts enjoyable and a little scary. But I guess that's what spending the day with a woman you're fighting an attraction to is like.

I'd almost convinced myself it wasn't an issue, but I can no longer deny it. My growing attraction to Aspen *is* a problem, and one I'm not sure how to deal with. Do I face it head-on like a man? Or admit defeat and remove myself from this situation?

After brushing my teeth and stripping down to my boxers, I climb under the blankets. In the quiet of my bedroom, my mind starts to wander. Aspen was so fucking cute on our hike. I have to fight off the mental image of her bare legs wearing only those damn white socks wrapped around my waist as I pummel into her.

It's then that everything crashes down on me at once. Because there's so much more to her than just her looks.

Aspen's words about her ex reaching out to her. Her ability to have fun even when everything in her life is uncertain. The way she's able to laugh and let go. I tend to spend a lot of time overthinking shit, but Aspen's the opposite. Once she works something out in her mind, she seems to move on. It's a good talent to have, I guess.

Another unique talent she has? Making my dick hard at the most inopportune times. Like earlier, when she placed her feet in my lap.

As I'm reliving that moment, the door opens slowly, and I lift my head from the pillow. The room is dark, but I have no problem making out Aspen's shadowy figure approaching my bed.

"Aspen?" My voice comes out hoarse. Is she sleep-walking? Scared of the dark?

"Sorry," she whispers. "Were you sleeping?" She pauses beside my bed and places one knee on the mattress.

I sit up. "Not yet. What's going on?"

"Can I join you?"

I open my mouth but nothing comes out. Aspen doesn't wait for my response, she just takes the spot on the bed next to me.

"What's up?" I ask as I scoot back a little and lean against the headboard.

She surprises me by crawling into my lap.

Whoa.

"My birthday's not over yet," she whispers. "And I was thinking about that time we kissed . . ."

I make an inarticulate sound. My body is a big fan of the way her soft curves feel in my lap, and my brain struggles to catch up.

"Aspen?" I groan. "You're kinda killing me here."

She smiles, and her tongue touches her lower lip. "Well, there's one more thing I wanted to do for my birthday. Birthday sex is a thing, you know?"

All the blood flow diverts from my brain, leaving me speechless. "Uh. Is it?"

When Aspen presses her lips to mine, I freeze. But only for a second because I can't help but respond to her kiss. As her mouth begins to move against mine, I devour her, my tongue stroking hers in hot devotion.

My hands curl into fists at my sides so I don't

touch her. Because what I want to do is fill my hands with that luscious ass of hers and drive my hips up.

Her lips move from mine down to my neck. I fight to ignore the hot lust that pulses low in my groin. I try to recall all the very valid reasons why hooking up with Aspen would be the worst idea ever, but I come up blank.

But she's been drinking, which means her decision-making might be impaired. Taking advantage of her is the last thing I want to do.

"Wait. Hold up." I touch her shoulder, and she pulls back.

In the shadowy bedroom, I can only just make out Aspen's eyes. They're hazy with desire, and her full, plush mouth is begging to be kissed.

Think, Braun. You can't do this.

"This isn't a good idea."

"I know," she says, running her hands over the muscles in my chest. "That's why I want to."

What the hell is that supposed to mean?

I groan out her name as her hands move over my bare skin.

"We should have sex," Aspen whispers, her hot

mouth pressed against my neck.

"We can't," I hear myself saying. *Thank God.* Because believe me, I want to nail her so damn hard. "You're drunk."

She lifts to her knees until we're eye to eye. "And if I wasn't?"

The weight of her ass is no longer pressed into my groin, but I still can't think straight for the life of me.

I scratch at the stubble on my jaw. The woman has a point. I inhale, fighting to get my libido under control. "What was all that stuff about nothing can happen between us?"

Aspen shrugs. "I don't know. Me being too . . . stuck up?"

I want to ask her what changed, but it's pointless. I've felt the growing attraction between us for days. Obviously, she has too, and now it seems she can no longer ignore it.

She moves from my lap to sit beside me. I reach under the blanket to adjust the growing situation in my boxers, and Aspen's mouth twitches with a knowing smile.

"For the record, I don't think this is a good idea. We're both coming off a bad breakup."

"Exactly." She nods. "Maybe a rebound fling is exactly what I need. We have the summer." Her nose scrunches. "Actually, we only have like twenty-four days left. We're here alone, away from the rest of the world, away from any distractions. We might as well make good use of the time."

I release a slow, strained exhale. "You make a damn convincing argument. But how about we wait and see how you feel in the morning?"

She gives me a crooked smile. "You suck, Braun."

"Believe me, I know." I chuckle darkly.

When she climbs from my bed, I do the gentlemanly thing and walk her back to her room, waiting by the door as she climbs into bed.

"Happy birthday, Aspen."

"Good night, party pooper," she says with a yawn.

When I get back in bed, I'm still as hard as a fence post in my boxers, and I know that trying to get to sleep is going to be nearly impossible. Maybe I'll have some interesting dreams tonight, where my restraint won't be quite so strong.

A man can hope.

• • •

The next morning I'm awoken by some bad news. The credit goes to a phone call from my lawyer bright and early. Apparently, a woman I met at a club last year is suing me for sexual harassment. I wish I was kidding.

After I pull on my sweatpants, I make my way downstairs and brew some coffee. I take my mug outside and call my agent. Aspen's still asleep, and I wouldn't want her to overhear this conversation anyway.

"What the hell do you mean they might drop me? It's your job to make sure that doesn't happen," I all but shout into the phone. "Do your fucking job."

My agent, Kyle, clears his throat.

After I filled him in on the charges, he informed me that my most lucrative sponsorship deal, one with Canada's largest sporting goods retailer, Rush Sports, might not wait for the dust to settle on this thing, or for the truth to come out. They might just decide I'm not worth the drama and negative press and drop me, rendering the million-dollar deal we've signed as useless as single-ply toilet paper.

It doesn't matter that the accusations about me

aren't true. As usual, I'm guilty until I prove my innocence.

"This is such bullshit," I grumble, shaking my head as my mood plummets.

Yes, I met this woman at a club last season, and I talked with her and her friend for a few minutes. I got the feeling she was interested in more, but I wasn't up for company that night.

That's the whole story. The absolute truth.

But she claims I promised her playoff tickets in exchange for sex, and then pressured her. I definitely didn't do that. But it's her word against mine, and with my reputation last season, people are probably going to believe her.

"We didn't even make the playoffs. Why would I promise someone tickets to something that didn't happen?"

"I know, Braun, calm down."

Calm down? Easy for him to say. Kyle's name isn't about to be trashed in the media. Eden will have my nuts if I bring more bad press to the team. *Fuck.*

"Breathe, Alex. I'm going to call your attorney when we hang up. See what we might be able to come up with. Maybe there's a creative solution."

"I sure as fuck hope so."

I pace back and forth on the deck, so pissed off, I'm seeing red. I would never, not in a million years, sexually harass or even proposition a woman unless I was sure she was one thousand percent interested.

Kyle goes on about getting this thing to go away quietly, as that would be the best for my reputation and brand partnerships.

"Yeah, and how would we accomplish that?"

"Easy, Alex. Money," he says.

"I'm not paying her one red cent. This is all fabricated. Did you not hear me the first time?"

"We might have to tread carefully here. You're not exactly the league's favorite player right now."

His words are a warning, reminding me that I'm walking a fine line.

I rub at my temples where a sudden headache is now forming. "Just do what you can. You need the contact info for my lawyer?"

"No, I've got it here," he says with a sigh. "Where are you?"

"Canada. Saint's lake house."

He makes a pensive noise. "Go paddleboarding or something. Try to relax. We'll talk when I know more."

Relax? Yeah, easy for him to say. "Right. Talk soon."

I'm still amped up and my coffee is now cold, but since it matches my mood, I drink it anyway. I sit down in one of the Adirondack chairs on the deck and take a long, bitter gulp.

This entire situation is fucked.

I look down at my phone and consider texting someone for advice. Saint? My sister? Maybe Coach Wilder? But that thought makes my stomach tighten even more, so I decide not to tell anyone. At least not now, not until I have to.

Kyle was right. I don't have the best reputation, and I don't like the thought that swirling doubts may overshadow my denial of this accusation. That there may be people out there, people in my own circle, who think that yeah, maybe I did do this shitty thing she says I did.

I sit here for a long time, until the goose bumps fade on my skin and my coffee mug is empty. But now I'm not thinking about lawyers or sexual harassment suits. I'm thinking about Aspen's come-on last night.

Unless I dreamed the entire thing—which, frankly, seems possible—I still can't quite believe how bold she was. Or how tempered I was. I'm normally impulsive.

The old Alex would have plowed through, doing whatever I wanted, letting the chips fall where they may. But the new Alex is all too aware that Aspen's career depends on my ex, and I don't want to mess anything up for her. It's obvious she's happy doing what she does and that she's got a good thing going with Eden, so I need to tread carefully.

My thoughts are interrupted by Aspen herself, who's wandered out on the deck to join me. She's showered, dressed, and wearing a bright smile.

"Good morning," she says, her tone chipper.

"Morning," I say in an equally gruff one.

Her gaze falls from mine and her smile fades as she focuses on the cup of coffee in her hands for a moment. "Is everything okay?"

"I was just making a phone call."

She takes a step back. "I see. Well, I'll just go back inside."

"Aspen, wait." I rise to my feet.

She inhales and shakes her head. "You don't

have to say anything. I'm sorry. Last night was my fault."

Her cheeks are pink with embarrassment, and my stomach drops. The last thing I want her to feel is ashamed. She read the situation between us right—I *do* want her. But now I'm in such a weird headspace, I'm blowing it.

"I didn't mean to upset you," she says, reaching for the door.

I take her wrist, stopping her, and turn her to face me. "You didn't upset me." Lowering my mouth to hers, I give her a slow, soft kiss. "My mood has nothing to do with you or with last night. I'm sorry if you thought otherwise."

Aspen blinks up at me. "Will you tell me what's bothering you?"

"Maybe another time." I touch her cheek. "I'd rather talk about your offer last night."

Her blush deepens and her eyes stray from mine. "Oh God, I was hoping I dreamed that."

I grin down at her. "And here I was hoping I didn't. Because your offer . . . a summer spent enjoying each other? Sounds hot as hell to me."

Her lips part and her wide eyes meet mine. A low thrum of desire pulses between us.

The memory of her in my bed last night is too powerful to shake. But something else, a twinge of conscience, pokes at me too. It wouldn't be fair to use Aspen to chase away all my troubles, even if I wanted to do exactly that.

But this was *her* idea. And if I could help her get that sparkle back in her eyes, and make her see just how desirable she is . . . wouldn't that be worth it?

She might have been drunk last night when she was brave enough to ask me for what she wanted. But there's no doubt in my mind that we've been building to this moment for the better part of a week.

Aspen is a good girl. Smart. Hard working. Ruled by her own common sense and self-preservation. But our chemistry is potent. And if she still wants this when she's sober? In the light of day? All bets are off.

When I lean down and take her mouth again, her lips part, inviting me in for a taste. I thread my fingers through her hair and touch my tongue to hers. A little whimper of surprise escapes before she begins kissing me back in earnest. She's skilled at this—her hot tongue matches mine stroke for stroke—and I have no doubt that things between us would be combustible.

Before I do something really stupid, like take her upstairs and pound out all of my pent-up energy, her phone makes a chirping noise. She pulls away.

"I have a call with Eden starting in a few minutes." Aspen is breathless, and I love the slightly dazed expression she wears.

I nod. "To be continued."

She gives me one more look of wanting, and then disappears inside to take that phone call.

10

ASPEN

My heart is still hammering in my ears when I sit down with my laptop at the dining room table and join the video call with Eden. Her face lights up my screen, her hair and makeup perfect, as usual. I absently touch my fingers to my mouth, my lips still tingling from the kiss I just shared with her ex.

I'm totally gonna lose my job over this.

"Hey, Aspen. How's cabin life treating you? You look great."

"Uh—it's . . ." I stumble over my words, completely sure that Eden's going to see right through me. "It's beautiful here. Saint has it made. The views alone are to die for."

"I'm jealous." She sighs with a small frown.

"Summer in the city can be suffocating. You're lucky you get to spend the hotter months where the air is fresh and doesn't smell like body odor."

I laugh at her description, because even though it sounds like a joke, it's actually true. "How's Holt?"

"Oh, you know. Stoic, somber. The usual." Eden's eyes sparkle with humor as she touches the engagement ring on her finger. You'd have to be blind to miss the look of adoration on her face, even as she teases her fiancé. "I think he misses having you around. He asked about you the other day. You know him—he's a protector, and he worries."

"Aw, that's so sweet." I chuckle, a little touched. Holt is the kind of guy who rarely smiles, unless the conversation is about Eden. So, for him to ask about me is surprisingly kind.

"I wish you weren't all alone out there," Eden says, her tone becoming serious for a moment.

My throat tightens. Wait. What? Doesn't she know Alex is here too?

"I half expected you to get ax-murdered by some Canadian mountain man before our first check-in," she says.

"No Canadian mountain men here. No, sirree."
I laugh, but it sounds thin and forced. I open my
planner, staring at the pages so I don't have to meet
her eyes. "Shall we get started?"

"Sure. So, I'm assuming you saw my email
about those invoices from last quarter . . ."

"I sure did. And I did some recon to find out
why they were screwy."

"Awesome." She grins. "I knew you'd figure
it out."

It's so easy to fall back into pace with Eden,
scribbling down abbreviated notes as she barrels
through a to-do list that might give a less-moti-
vated assistant an aneurysm. She's a wonderful
boss—always making her priorities clear without
being condescending, and never fails to compli-
ment a job well done. Ever since I started this job,
our working relationship has been smooth sailing.
I'd hate for anything to rock the boat.

And by anything, I mean a hulking, hotter-than-
hell hockey player who happens to be her ex, and
who I'm very likely going to have sex with before
the end of the summer. Repeatedly.

Suddenly, Eden pauses mid-thought. "Is that
Alex?"

My gasp is audible. I look up from my planner so fast that I nearly give myself whiplash. Sure enough, Alex is walking across the deck in the background of my setup, totally oblivious to his brief on-screen cameo. And to make matters worse, he's shirtless.

Shit.

"Yeah," I say lamely. It seems that all my coherent thoughts have disappeared, and probably took with them all the color in my face. "Um, yeah, so he's also staying here at the cabin."

Eden's eyes widen more than I thought was possible. "Why the hell is he staying there?"

"Funny story . . . he was the one who got me the job in the first place, 'cause it was supposed to be his, but then he, uh, recommended *me* for it, and actually there's a *lot* more manual labor than you'd think, so Saint suggested we split up the workload." I paraphrase poorly, rushing everything out in one breath. I always ramble when I'm nervous.

Eden tilts her head, her mouth opening and closing like a very confused, very irritated fish. "Does he always walk around with his shirt off?"

I choke out a laugh. "N-no . . ." My fingers twitch at the memory of how strong his bare chest felt when it flexed under my touch last night, with

Alex pinned between my legs. The way he hardened and swelled against my ass when I—

"Anything happening there?" she asks, her big blue eyes narrowing with suspicion. Leave it to Eden Wynn to cut to the chase. The woman is known to be direct, and she doesn't disappoint.

"Me and Alex? No." I scoff, lying so easily to the woman who signs my paycheck that I almost believe it myself.

"Okay, good," she murmurs, lowering her voice. "He's trouble, Aspen." Her tone is softer now, less accusatory. "I wouldn't want to see you get hurt. You've already been through so much. Is he at least behaving himself?"

"Yeah, he's been very respectful. We're getting along fine."

Eden's eyebrows jump. "You've been hanging out, then?"

I nod, afraid to say anything more. If I do, I might confess the whole crime.

Crime? I've done nothing wrong, so why do I feel like I'm being interrogated?

"Correct me if I'm wrong," Eden says, "but I thought you were going up there to recoup, sweetie. And now you're sleeping under the same roof as the enemy?"

Alex doesn't feel like the enemy. Not to me, anyway. "It's been fine, Eden. I promise."

She shakes her head, concern creasing her brow. "You say that now. He's probably still on his best behavior. Just wait. Please call me if anything changes. If he becomes an ass, I want to know about it. I'm saying that as your boss and your friend."

My gut clenches uncomfortably at the genuine concern in her eyes. Eden was with Alex for a really long time, so it's safe to assume that she knows the man better than I do. How hurt would she be if she found out about our little arrangement?

I'm not looking for a relationship with the guy or anything, but sex has a nasty habit of complicating dynamics, especially in the workplace. Being at a remote cabin has made it so easy to distance myself from reality. Is sleeping with Alex really worth risking the last bit of stability I have left in my life?

Ugh. My brain is one big scrambled egg. I'm sure the answer is *no*, but my body is screaming for me to do it.

Before Eden can notice me spiraling, I smile. "I'll be okay. I'm a big girl, I promise. Anyway, don't you have another call soon?"

Eden gasps, glancing down at her dainty gold wristwatch. "In five minutes, actually." Her sigh is exasperated but her smile is soft. "Thanks for always keeping me on track, Aspen. Think we can touch base again like this next week? Or sooner, you know . . ." She trails off with a look that says, *if Alex gives you any trouble.*

"Works for me. 'Bye, boss."

"'Bye, girl."

Eden signs off, and I close my laptop.

Little does she know, Alex may be giving me a whole lot more than trouble this summer. Like multiple orgasms, if we make good on our arrangement.

I chew my lip, twisting in my seat to peer out the window. Alex is hosing down the deck, a fresh sheen of sweat making his burly chest and arm muscles glisten in the sun.

How am I supposed to make any headway on my to-do list when he's looking like *that*? We're gonna need to enforce a stricter clothing policy if we intend to get *any* work done this month.

Even though it may not be my brightest idea, hooking up seems unavoidable at this point. I pretty much blew the lid off that can of worms when

I drunkenly climbed onto his lap last night. And judging by his reaction this morning, it doesn't seem like this sexual frustration is going anywhere unless we channel it in a more productive way.

Heck, maybe if we explore our attraction for each other *now*, we'll be tired of each other by the time the season begins. After all, what happens in Canada, stays in Canada, right?

Is it naive to think that way? Can I trust Alex to be professional and keep our secret when the season begins?

Eden had me conditioned into thinking Alex was a loose cannon, moody and selfish. And maybe he was. Before.

But the man who gave up his summer plans for me? The man who gave me an unforgettable birthday? The guy who helped that dad and his kid at the grocery store? That's not the Alex I was told to watch out for. Now that I know him better, it seems like his whole world was upended after the breakup. It wouldn't surprise me if losing a girl like Eden left a mark. Heartbreak changes people. At the very least, I owe it to Alex to decide for myself without influence from anyone else.

Actually, I owe it to *myself*.

How many times have I set aside my own desires just to keep the peace? By the end of our relationship, my ex had me convinced that I couldn't physically come anymore because I was somehow broken. Too stressed, too picky. Damaged goods. It never occurred to him that maybe the sex with him was just bad.

You know who probably isn't bad at sex? *Alex Braun.*

My libido might as well be screaming his name, begging me to shed my inhibitions already. Besides, Alex needs a discreet rebound, away from the cameras and tabloids, and I need someone to screw me senseless. Seems like a mutually beneficial arrangement.

Now I've just got to be brave enough to rock the boat.

11

ALEX

I've just finished today's chores when my phone rings again.

"How was the paddleboarding?" Kyle asks when I answer his call.

I scoff. "Fuck off with the niceties. You know I didn't go paddleboarding. Now tell me what's going on."

He releases a low chuckle. "So, I talked to Hugh. Nice guy, by the way. And if this breaks, Rush Sports is going to pull the deal. That's a given. Nothing we can do about that."

I pace the deck, my phone in a death grip. "That *can't* happen. I'm not going to lose out on a million-dollar deal because this chick decided to tell a lie."

"It's tough, I know. Believe me. Nasty publicity isn't the end of the world, though. This kind of thing can be great for a book deal. That's something we can discuss down the road."

"Do you even hear yourself talking?"

Kyle has the audacity to laugh. "Easy, buddy. You haven't exactly been the golden boy the league assumed you were. First the messy breakup with the team owner, then a rocky season, and now this? Dude, you're sort of the 2007 Britney of the NHL. Just don't shave your hair on camera anytime soon."

"What the fuck? I worked my ass off last season."

"I know, but you were also down in goals and assists. And you were photographed with plenty of women. Opinions about you are being formed. Hang tight. I'm going to try to get these allegations to go away."

Anger boils inside me. "I'm not paying her. She's a liar."

"We'll see. Sometimes it's worth it to throw a little money at these situations."

That tension headache from earlier is back with a vengeance. "You know I didn't do this, Kyle."

I've worked with the guy for three years now, and I would hope he knows I'm not a womanizing scumbag.

"I don't care if you did it or not." He laughs again. "If you ask me, some of these women are asking for it."

"Are you being serious right now? No woman is *asking* to be sexually harassed."

Kyle makes a noncommittal sound.

What the hell? Not only do I have to deal with this lawsuit, but now I've got to find a new agent on top of that? Fuck me.

I've put up with his insensitive cracks and disgusting jokes for three years now. I guess when someone shows you their true colors, you should believe them.

When I end the call, I'm determined to leave all this messy shit behind me. At least for today. It's unfortunately not possible to do it for good, though. I mean, I'm not *that* optimistic.

But Aspen doesn't deserve my crappy mood. None of this is her fault, and I'll have plenty of time to worry, dissect, and stew over it. Just not today. Today, I want to go make a pretty girl smile.

And it turns out, it's not that difficult to achieve.

A little while later, Aspen appears. She's such a bright, sunny spot for me this summer, that my entire mood changes.

"Hey," I say less than smoothly. "Your call go okay?"

"Yup." She nods. "It went well. All done with work for the day too."

I nod. I wonder if she told Eden that I'm here, but I guess it doesn't matter. Aspen and I are adults, and whatever happens next is just between us.

My heart rate kicks up as we stand in the living room, silently watching each other. I can't help but think about our kiss this morning, and the promise of it *to be continued*.

Does Aspen still want that too?

"Let's go for a swim," I say. I'm sweaty and hot, and although the water is probably freezing, maybe that's just what I need to douse my raging libido.

"Let's do it," she says brightly.

After changing into my swimming shorts, I wait for her on the dock. A moment later, she appears. Her bathing suit is a two piece, basic black with a halter top that ties behind her neck. She looks delicious, all smooth skin and creamy curves. Her body is just as a woman's should be. Soft and luscious.

All my irritated thoughts from earlier fly away. Right now, all I want now is to forget about everything and indulge in her.

When Aspen tries to cover herself with the towel, I tug it away playfully. "Don't do that. You're perfect."

One eyebrow arches as she watches me. "I'm not. But thank you."

"How do you want to do this? It's going to be cold," I warn her.

She drops her towel and dips one toe into the dark blue water, fighting off a shiver. "It's freezing."

"Cannonball?" Smirking, I raise a brow at her.

"I think that's the only way." She grins and reaches for my hand.

All at once, and with a running start, we hold hands and jump in together. The icy water steals the breath from my lungs, and when we surface, Aspen lets out a shriek.

"Holy shit, that's freezing."

I laugh. "I told you."

She shivers and treads water, humming to distract herself.

"Come here," I say, opening my arms to her.

Aspen fits herself against me, and suddenly I'm no longer cold. Her soft curves press to my chest, and she feels warm in my arms.

"That's better," she murmurs, looking up to gaze at me.

She wraps her legs around my waist and releases a strained exhale. When her eyes meet mine, they're filled with desire, and my heart nearly explodes.

I know she can feel me hardening, despite the freezing water. As my cock juts out and presses against her ass, her eyes widen and meet mine. "Sorry," I mumble, but she doesn't look bothered by this.

So I kiss her. Slowly. Adoringly. Our lips connecting lazily before gently retreating again. But my slow exploration doesn't last long, because I feel the warmth of Aspen's fingers threading into the hair at the back of my neck, and then her lips part.

I taste her with measured strokes of my tongue against hers as my breathing quickens. Rocking my hips against her center elicits another of those strained sounds from her. It's an unspoken promise between us. I would be happy to fuck her into next Tuesday, but not until she's ready.

"Soon," I whisper.

Her mouth fuses to mine again, and our kiss deepens. Her hand brushes the front of my shorts, and my cock jerks.

"Maybe we should go inside," she says on a shaky exhale.

Five little words. That's all it takes to make me lose my resolve.

While she clings to me, I swim us with one arm back to the ladder attached to the dock, but if Aspen notices my awkward swimming technique, she doesn't comment on it. She climbs out first and grabs her towel, wrapping herself securely.

The cold water has done nothing to temper my raging erection, and as I climb out behind her, her gaze falls to the place where my shorts are wildly tented in front of me. I should feel embarrassed. I'm like a horny teenager who can't control his body, but when her cheeks brighten, all I feel is prideful lust.

I tug on a T-shirt and wrap myself in a towel,

and then we jog toward the house. Inside and up the stairs, we leave a dripping trail of water in our wake. At the top of the stairs, Aspen tugs my hand.

I follow her to her bedroom. The bed is bigger in this room and it's neatly made. I spin her in my arms and kiss her again as our towels fall into a damp heap at our feet.

Aspen pulls back and offers me a shy smile. "I'll be right back. Make yourself comfortable."

I release a slow exhale and nod. She disappears into the bathroom, which gives me a minute to think.

I don't know how far she intends on going today, but the decision I made to leave the condoms at home suddenly seems like a very, very stupid one. Maybe there's a random one still in my duffel bag?

But no, it's wishful thinking. I know there's not. And the nearest store is a good forty-plus minutes away. That's nearly two hours there and back . . . which would totally ruin the mood. *Fuck.*

Sprinting across the hall, I do the only thing I can think to do with all the blood in my body rushing south. I grab my phone and text Saint.

Hey . . . uh, you have any prophylactics

here, by chance?

Pro-what? he replies a second later.

Saint's dumb ass probably doesn't know the meaning of the word . . . or how to spell it.

I peek across the hall. The bathroom door is still closed, and I hear running water.

Condoms. It almost pains me to type the word because it means Saint now knows our personal business. But desperate times and all that jazz.

He sends back the emoji of the purple-faced devil with a smirking grin. This is amazing. You are such a fuckup.

Do you or not? I text back.

Master closet. Top shelf. I can't wait to pick out your new tattoo. You kids have fun!

I pull open the closet door and help myself to a square foil packet. Happy with the expiration date, I set it on the dresser just as Aspen opens the door and reenters the bedroom.

I swallow a wave of nerves. I woke up the last three mornings with my hand inside my boxers, stroking my dick while I dreamed about being buried inside Aspen, convinced that it could never really happen. But now that the moment is here, I'm more uncertain than ever.

When she steps into my arms again, she chases away the cold. Our skin may still be raised in chill bumps, but I'm hot all over.

With trembling fingers, I untie the strings securing the top of her bikini. Her breasts are perky and perfect, and I trace her nipples with my thumbs. She inhales a shaky breath as I explore her body . . . the dip in her belly, the weight of her breasts in my hands, the soft, want-filled sounds she makes when I pinch her nipples.

Aspen trails her fingers along my bicep. "Tell me what you like. In bed, I mean. I'm worried I won't—"

"Don't worry about a thing. I like *you*."

And with that, she kisses me. *Hard*.

I force a long, slow breath into my lungs and try not to get too excited. Which is difficult, because I haven't had sex in months. So this is either going to go really, really good . . . or really, really fast.

When she tugs off my T-shirt, it doesn't feel like she's just removing my clothes. It feels like she's removing my armor, freeing me, layer by layer, of whatever it was that was holding me back before. And being bare-chested with her, holding her close? It's magic. Her soft breasts press into the hard planes of my chest, and I can feel the frantic rhythm of her heart. Mine's beating just as fast.

When we part, she gives my chest an appraising stare, her eyes lowering as she takes in my physique. I work hard for it. Sometimes it feels nice to be noticed. To be seen. And Aspen sees me.

"Your body is insane," she murmurs, trailing her fingertips over the grooves between my abs. Her fingertips linger over the black heart tattooed on my chest. I could stand here and let her admire me like this, but my body has other ideas.

I guide her to the bed, and when she sits and begins scooting up toward the pillows, I hook my fingers into her bikini bottoms and tug. As badly as my body aches for her touch, my need to watch her come apart is even greater.

When she parts her knees, I climb toward her, appreciating the delicious view of pink, wet flesh that I want to devour.

My cock is still very hard and *very* ready for

fucking, but I take my time, kissing a path from her knee up to her core. I press my mouth to her center and use my tongue to stroke her clit. The sound Aspen makes is surprised and pleasure filled. I don't stop until she sinks her fingers into my hair and comes apart, her body jerking as her orgasm washes over her.

After, I settle next to her, kissing her neck, and she reaches between us to untie the laces holding my swim shorts together.

"You sure you want this?"

Aspen licks her lower lip and nods, and there's not a single doubt in her eyes. "Positive."

The word crashes through me. "Then take out my cock."

Her hand dips beneath the waistband to draw out my aching erection. My eyes sink closed and my jaw clenches as she curls her fist around me and begins to stroke.

With one delicate fingertip, she traces a vein in my cock with the lightest touch, but I feel it everywhere.

I can't take it anymore. I shove the damp shorts the rest of the way off and toss them to the floor.

"Condom." I croak out the word, my voice now

rough with need.

I tip my chin to the dresser, and Aspen retrieves the foil packet, tearing it open with nimble fingers. She hands the condom to me, and I sheath myself in a matter of seconds.

I move between her legs and align us, balancing my weight on my forearms. She can't seem to stop herself from touching me, though. Running her hands over the muscles in my ass. Cupping the back of my neck so I'll lean in and kiss her. Palming my biceps and appreciating the way they tense as I hover over her. I love it.

Part of me could stay here in this moment forever, kissing Aspen and letting her touch me, but the organ below my navel has other ideas. My cock ruts and nudges against her, insistently asking to be let in.

She says my name with desperation, and it's good to know I'm not the only one who feels so desperately out of control.

When I press forward, I'm welcomed into the slick heat of her body with a soft moan.

"Okay?" I check in, pausing but not withdrawing.

"One second." She nods, her breath sawing in

and out of her unevenly as she adjusts to the intrusion of my body into hers.

I sense that this is more than just sex to Aspen. There's some reclaiming of herself, some rebuilding of her broken self-confidence. It's beautiful to watch. I know the feeling. I need a moment to right myself too, because this feels too good to be true.

She relaxes, her fingers pressing into my shoulder. I thrust again, sinking into her heat until there's no space left between us.

"Fuck," I grunt out. "You're tight."

I bury my face into her neck and breathe in her scent. She smells of lavender and rainwater and the sweet scent of female. And then she starts to move against me, lifting her hips to meet my thrusts.

I've bedded a lot of women, but suddenly my mind goes blank of everyone before her. I can't recall a single one of them, not even if you paid me a million dollars.

All I can think of is Aspen. Aspen with her pouting mouth and flushed cheeks. Aspen with those wide blue eyes trained on mine, and her lush curves, and the scent of her desire. The wet spot she's currently leaving on the sheets as I fuck her tight, curvy body.

She's drenching me in her heat, and I can't take much more. She feels unbearably good, and my self-control is shot.

"I need to come," I say on a growl.

"*Yes*. I'm close," she murmurs.

It's only a few whispered syllables, but to me, they mean so much. The fact that she's choosing to be here with me, giving herself to me so completely, makes my heart swell in a way I'm not sure it has before.

I bring one hand between us, and when I touch her slick heat, Aspen curses—pushing out words I've never heard leave her mouth before—and her body quakes around mine. Her climax is powerful, stealing the breath from my lungs and squeezing my cock in hot, pulsing waves until I have no choice but to follow her over the edge.

With a low groan, I fill the condom with my release. It's the most powerful orgasm of my life, and my hips jerk up in a hard thrust as I bury myself inside her for a final time.

Holy shit. What was that?

I move off her, rolling to my side, though I immediately miss the heat of her skin, the weight of my body pressing hers into the soft mattress. My heart rate slows, and I press a kiss to her temple. "That was incredible."

Aspen merely nods, her eyes heavy and her expression one of total satisfaction. With one last look of appreciation, I exit the bed.

It's then that I notice the light has changed. It's no longer afternoon, and the room is painted in orange and pink twilight.

Inside the bathroom, I dispose of the condom and wash my hands, and when I reenter the bedroom, I try to get a read on the situation. Does she want me to grab my clothes and go? Is she done with me now? I mean, it was just a hookup, so I'd get it if she wanted her space to herself now.

But her face is relaxed and open, and she pats the spot on the bed next to her.

With a smile, I climb in once again, covering us with the sheet. She curls into my side, using my chest as her pillow, and I bring one arm around her to hold her close.

While we lie there together, we talk of many things. First, about mundane things like how awful that freezing-cold lake water was, and about the things I'm going to make her for dinner while we're here. But we dive into weightier things too. She tells me about losing her father when she was twelve to a drunk driver, and I tell her of almost losing my mom to breast cancer ten years ago.

They're heavy topics, but with Aspen curled up on the bed beside me, my fingertips lazily tracing circles onto the skin of her shoulder, they don't feel so insurmountable. It feels natural to be sharing the deepest parts of ourselves after something so intimate.

And I realize with a jolt of clarity, that might be the most dangerous thing of all.

12

ASPEN

"**W**hy does everything taste better after sex?" I ask between doughy bites.

Alex found the waffle maker in one of the cupboards this morning before I even got out of bed. I'll admit, it was kind of disappointing to wake up and roll over, only to find an empty pillow. Even if the sex is the best sex you've ever had, I'm pretty sure if a guy goes MIA the morning after sleeping with you for the first time, that's not a great sign. But this syrupy breakfast is doing a good job of making up for it, so all is forgiven.

"Endorphins," Alex says, but something's missing in his voice. His usual sense of humor is gone, replaced with an undercurrent of tension.

That's . . . *weird*. Maybe I'm reading into it.

I wash down my last bite with a sip of coffee. "Did you sleep all right?"

"Fine," he mutters, his gaze glued to the table.

Has he looked at me even *once* this morning? Dread settles around me like a wet coat. Something's definitely wrong.

"Are you okay?" I meekly reach out to brush the back of his hand with my fingertips.

Alex almost flinches away before he seems to make the decision to take my hand firmly in his. I'm trying to decipher his serious expression when he finally makes eye contact, his gaze stormy.

"Can we talk?" he asks, his voice flat and emotionless.

Okay, I'm definitely *not* reading into it. My stomach drops. "Of course."

The muscle in Alex's jaw ticks like he's gritting his teeth. I brace for impact.

"I think last night was a mistake."

The word *mistake* crash-lands on the table between us. Bracing didn't help. I'm stunned.

"A mistake?" I repeat the words numbly. "It seemed to me like you had a good time."

"I did." He sighs, squeezing my hand.

I pull back, knotting my fingers in my lap. I don't want his pity. I want an explanation.

"And that's the problem," he says. "I always do this. Jump in without thinking about the consequences. Anything for a good time, right? But then my impulsiveness bites me in the ass. It always ends the same."

Blinking rapidly, I try to process it all. Where has this come from? "What are you saying, Alex?"

"I'm saying that last night was a one-time deal. It won't happen again. It can't."

I saw it coming, but that doesn't take away the sting of his words. I break away from his penetrating gaze and opt to stare out the window. "Well, isn't that convenient. You get to make all the decisions, and I get to live with all the regret."

Alex shakes his head. "I don't regret it, Aspen. Not one bit. And I hope you don't either, but I can't tell you how you should or shouldn't feel." He rakes his fingers through his hair, his eyes squeezed shut. "I'm trying so hard *not* to be an asshole for once in my life. I'm trying to do the right thing."

"And what's the right thing?"

He opens his eyes, pinning me in place. "I want

to be your friend, Aspen. Not your fuck buddy."

"So, you didn't like fucking me?" The word feels stilted and unfamiliar on my tongue. But it packs a necessary punch.

"Of course I did. Fuck, Aspen. Last night was . . ." He trails off. It was a lot of fun. Really."

Fun. I guess that makes me the girl you have *fun* with once, and then immediately discard. Good for a one-night stand and nothing else. What did I expect?

I bite my lip, blinking back hot, angry tears. *I will not cry.* I've dealt with rejection far worse than this, so I will *not* cry. Especially not in front of him.

Alex's chair creaks as he slumps back. "I'm sorry. Really, I am."

"Fine. If that's what you want, then it's fine, Alex." I don't know how I manage to say that so evenly, but I do. Even though the weight of all these tears I refuse to cry may crush me.

A long, excruciating pause stretches between us before he speaks again. "Thanks, Aspen."

Alex clears his side of the table quickly and quietly before he leaves the room, muttering something about the guesthouse and clogged gutters.

I almost want to yell after him, *Good. You should probably stay in the guesthouse anyway.* But all the wind has already been knocked out of me, and I don't think I could speak right now, even if I wanted to.

I try to keep my mind blank, washing the dishes by hand and scrubbing every possible surface of the kitchen until it's squeaky clean. Then I move into the pantry for today's task—taking inventory and throwing out anything that's expired. Between the clatter of canned goods being tossed in the trash, Eden's words ring hollowly in my mind.

"He's trouble, Aspen. I wouldn't want to see you get hurt."

Who did I think I was, questioning her advice? Eden was the person closest to Alex for five freaking years. She knows him better than anyone, and me? I've barely known the man five minutes, and I trusted him with my . . . well, with everything.

"I want to be your friend, Aspen. Not your fuck buddy."

I check the expiration date of a can of tomato soup, but my brain is so rattled, I don't even know what year it is anymore.

Alex said he was trying to do the right thing. Why does the "right thing" have to be abstaining from really awesome sex? I finally allowed myself to trust my gut, to *take* what I want, and this is how it works out for me? Old Aspen was on to something with her impossibly high walls and unshakable professionalism.

You'd think that escaping alone to the Canadian wilderness wouldn't lead to even more heartache. But here I am, trying not to let some guy make me cry all over again.

13

ALEX

I kick a bucket into the corner and let out a frustrated growl. I've been outside in the shed, not exactly hiding, but . . .

Okay, fine. I'm hiding.

But *fuck*. How is it that I manage to mess something up so horribly when all I'm trying to do is the right thing?

The hurt look on Aspen's face when I told her last night had been a mistake haunts me.

I want to kick my own ass. That was a shittier thing to do than what Dale did to her. Why did I have to call what we shared a mistake? Of all the words I could have used.

The nonstop barrage of texts from Saint this morning hasn't helped either.

After one of the best nights of my life, I got up early and made coffee. While I waited for Aspen to wake up, I checked in with my lawyer to see if there were any updates. There weren't any updates on the case, but that didn't stop him from pointing out that now would be a very bad time to get involved with someone new. He said the smartest thing to do would be to stay single this summer and keep my relationships out of the press, and that meant not being seen with any new women.

After that text, the texts from Saint started.

He had a field day, firing off a bunch of tattoo options he has for me. Every one of them is atrocious. From the elaborate face of a troll eating oatmeal that I won't be able to scrub from my brain anytime soon, to something simple like his name in a fancy font. Or my personal favorite, a block-text banner that read I'M AN IDIOT. Because that's exactly what I am. A gigantic fucking idiot.

I, of course, shot off my own texts, arguing that the tattoo was only if I fell in love, and Aspen and I had hooked up *once*. So I told him to fuck off.

But the truth is, I can picture a life with Aspen. And that's probably what scares me more than anything, because I seem to have a knack for destroying everything in my path.

Deciding I can't hide out in the shed forever, I grab the batteries I came looking for and make my way back inside. I keep myself busy by checking all the smoke detectors, but our dance around the cabin gets harder. When I hear her in the kitchen, I make myself scarce, and when she hangs out in the living room, I head out to the deck.

But I can't avoid her forever—not when we're living under the same roof. I do my best to busy myself with tasks today, but when Aspen walks into a room, all my attention is shot. She's all I can focus on.

It's now late in the afternoon, and she's wrapped herself in a fuzzy throw blanket and is stationed on the couch. She's down to the last dozen or so pages of her novel. Her mouth is turned down, and she hasn't even looked up to acknowledge my presence all day. I want to ask her about the ending, but I don't dare.

After I return the ladder to the garage, I pause in the living room. "Anything in particular sound good for dinner?"

She looks up at me with a frown. "I'm not hungry."

Okay. I deserved that. She's not even going to grace me with her presence, or share a meal with me anymore. The realization that she won't be making those little noises of satisfaction when I feed her does nothing to improve my mood.

When I don't move, Aspen looks up and meets my gaze. Even though she's obviously mad at me, I can still feel the familiar buzz of chemistry crackling between us.

Last night was intense, more intimate than a hookup had any right to be. Saint's words ring in my head. *"She's the marrying kind, bro. So unless you're trying to become someone's husband, it means you'd better keep your dick in your pants this summer."*

If only I'd listened. The last thing I need is a wife. If I know one thing for certain, it's that I'd be a terrible partner. I think about the strained relationship of my parents. It took my mom getting cancer for them to finally sort their shit out. And they did, but just barely.

Ending things between Aspen and me was the right thing to do.

Wasn't it?

And there's another factor at play here too. I can't risk pissing off Eden. I had big hopes for this season, and now I'm going to be facing down some lawsuit in court too—because I refused to settle or accept blame for something I didn't do. I have to tread carefully. Hooking up with my boss's assistant and friend? Not in the cards for someone trying to walk the straight and narrow.

Aspen's gaze falls from mine and returns to her book. The sting of her rejection, which I'm definitely not accustomed to, hurts more than I care to admit.

"Hey, uh, can we talk? When you're done with your book?"

She looks down, seeming to realize for the first time that she's on the last few pages, and then back up at me. "Sure."

"On the deck. Maybe fifteen minutes?"

"Okay," she says, but there's no joy in her voice.

Fifteen minutes later, true to her word, Aspen joins me outside on the deck.

I've lifted the cover off the hot tub and stored it on the side of the house. A bottle of wine and a single wineglass rest on a small table beside the sunken hot tub—along with a plate of cheese and crackers, and a bunch of purple grapes.

"What's this?" she asks, stopping like she's afraid to come any closer.

"For you. I've heated it so it should be warm." I tip my chin toward the hot tub, which bubbles and steams in the cooling, early evening air. "It's my attempt at apologizing," I say sheepishly. "I never meant to upset you."

Aspen nods once. "Is that my dinner?" She eyes the wine and platter I've prepared for her.

"If you want it to be."

"Thank you," she says, wandering closer. She dips her fingers into the water to test the temperature and makes a pleased sound. Saint told me this thing heats fast, and I'm glad he wasn't wrong. "I guess I'll get my suit on."

When she turns for the door, she pauses and then faces me again. "For the record, you didn't *upset* me. But you did make me feel like I was nothing more than a used Kleenex. So, yeah."

I wince. "I am *so* sorry about that. I promise that was *not* my intention. I fucked up. Majorly."

She nods in agreement and then disappears inside to change into her swimsuit.

A few minutes later, Aspen returns dressed in a fluffy white bathrobe and a pair of pink slippers. When she unties the robe and slides it off her shoulders, I nearly swallow my tongue. Because *damn*, *she does not fight fair.* She's wearing a bright red one-piece that dips low in front to show off her ample cleavage.

I make myself scarce while she disrobes and climbs into the warm water. Mentally, I'm not strong enough to watch that play out. The sound of relief pushing past her lips makes my balls ache.

Once she's submerged, I pour her a glass of wine and hand it to her. "Thanks," she murmurs. Then I gather some towels and set them beside the hot tub in a chair.

"Okay. Enjoy. I'm going to go make a sandwich or something."

She nods, and I head for the door, but before I reach it, she clears her throat.

"Alex?"

I turn around quickly. "Yes?"

"Thanks. And, um, if you want to join me . . . there's plenty of room." As if to prove her point, she wiggles her toes on the far end of the hot tub.

"You sure?" I ask, surprise filling my tone. My God, this is such a bad idea, stacked on top of my last bad idea. But I can hardly bring myself to care.

She nods.

Before she can change her mind, I dash upstairs and strip out of my clothes so fast, I practically set a world record. Less than a minute later, I'm easing into the water beside her, while Aspen makes an amused noise that sounds a lot like laughter.

The top of her breasts are visible in the water, and I force my eyes away, but it's too late. I can't exactly help the fact that my dick is now hard.

Terrific. The little fucker has terrible timing. It's not like I can climb out of the hot tub right now and go jerk off . . . or ask Aspen to take care of it. Although, the idea of that is more than a little arousing. Aspen's small, manicured hand being the one to work my dick, rather than my own calloused one.

Down, boy. That ship has sailed.

In fact, you torpedoed it. *Dumbass*.

"This is nice," she says, leaning her head against the edge of the hot tub and closing her eyes briefly.

"Yeah. And . . ." I release a slow exhale and her eyes open, finding mine. "I really am sorry. The truth is, I don't know why I said the shit I did this morning. I enjoyed every single thing about last night."

Aspen brings her wineglass to her lips, watching me. Waiting for me to continue.

"And I guess I just thought, let's leave it there, with a happy memory to remember it by. I didn't want to mess that up."

"Okay," she says softly.

"In case you haven't heard—I'm a fuckup. So, messing up somehow was inevitable."

She shifts. "Do you really believe that?"

I reach for the bottle and refill her glass. "I don't know. If history is any indication, then yeah."

Her expression is contemplative. "Want some?" Aspen offers me her glass.

"Do you think I'm a dick?" I ask, accepting the glass.

Her eyes narrow as she watches me take a sip of the wine. "I don't think you're a dick, Alex."

My relief at those words is immediate, and I relax, sinking a few inches lower into the water.

We share the bottle of wine, both of us drinking from her glass as we make small talk. Between the wine and the fact that Aspen that seems to have forgiven me, I'm lulleds into actually relaxing.

Later, when we're thoroughly pruned from the hot water, I cover the hot tub and make us something to eat while Aspen goes off to shower and change.

As we're sitting at the kitchen island eating grilled cheese sandwiches, I remind her about the youth hockey camp I'm helping with in New York next weekend.

"Will your nephew be there?"

I shake my head. "He's too little. This camp is for ages ten and up, but I'll be sure to see him while I'm there."

Aspen's dressed in gray knit pants and a long-sleeved pink T-shirt. She's not wearing a bra beneath it, and I'm trying hard not to notice. I finish my food and rinse my plate.

"Well, I think I'm going to call it a night," she says, rising to her feet. "Thanks for the sandwich."

"Anytime. Good night." I watch her head off up the stairs, then finish tidying up the kitchen.

When I make it upstairs a few minutes later, the light in her bedroom is still on, but I don't dare venture closer to investigate. Aspen may have forgiven me, but that doesn't mean we'll be having a repeat of last night.

No matter how desperately I might want to.

14

ASPEN

My bare feet carry me down the hall as unease swims inside me. *What am I doing?*

Against all self-preservation. Against all sense of logic and common sense. And even at the risk of enduring terrible heartache later, I stand here at Alex's open bedroom door, waiting for an invitation inside.

He's shirtless, dressed only in a pair of gray joggers that hang low on his trim waist. He meets my eyes.

"Thanks for earlier." My voice is a little shaky. "The hot tub was nice."

"Yeah, it was. And you're welcome."

"So was the apology."

He runs one hand over the back of his neck, and I admire the way his bicep flexes. "I was wrong, just so you know. Last night wasn't a mistake." His deep voice rumbles over the words.

"Are you sure about that?"

He nods. "Positive."

I take a step closer, entering his room, and my heart begins to pound wildly.

Before I have the chance to chicken out, Alex closes the distance between us, his powerful body moving with confidence until he stops directly in front of me. Using two fingers beneath my chin, he lifts my mouth to his. His lips are warm and soft—but insistent.

My entire body tingles, and my core aches with desire as I lose myself to this moment. His mouth moves with the deliberate, hot strokes of his tongue. I love it, craving more. I've never been kissed like this, and I hold nothing back.

When my hands grip his shoulders, tugging him closer, he begins to touch me. He slides his palms beneath my T-shirt to caress and tease my breasts, then lower, into the back of my pants, which he pushes out of the way as he slides his hands along the curve of my ass.

"Is this okay?" he asks between blazing-hot kisses.

I make a noise of approval, and Alex sinks to his knees. On his way down, he kisses my neck, my chest, my navel. And with my pants now around my ankles, he brings his mouth to the apex of my thighs and treats my center to a slow, sensuous kiss.

I moan, and my eyes close as I fist his hair.

"You taste so *fucking* good." He groans, devouring me in hot, wet kisses.

My legs tremble, and I try to steady myself with one hand on the wall behind me, and one on his shoulder.

His face lifts to mine. "Let's move to the bed."

I step out of my tangled pants and let him guide me to the mattress.

I'm not sure what brought me to Alex's room tonight. He already told me it couldn't happen again, shouldering all the blame for the reasons why it couldn't.

But our sexual encounter last night seemed to have awakened something deep inside me. I couldn't get enough of him. The way he looked at me. The sexy hair on his chest. His huge hands. His muscled body. I want it all. Again. And again. And he doesn't seem to notice or care about the extra twenty pounds I could stand to lose. He made me feel desirable. Wanted. *Needed*.

Part of me knows that he was right—maybe we shouldn't indulge in each other this way.

Except there's another part of me who's tired of playing it safe. A part of me who knows that sticking by Dale's side for all those years did absolutely nothing for me. So, it's *this* voice I listen to—this confident, brazen, sexual side of me that's saying things like, *YES, GIRL. It's more than okay to bang the hot hockey player for no other reason than the fact that you want to.*

And looking into Alex's dark blue eyes now, heavy with arousal, I realize I was crazy to think that things were actually over between us.

Especially with so much summer left.

15

ALEX

I messed things up once already, but we could only stand the blistering chemistry between us for so long. And it seems that Aspen has reached her limit. I'm just lucky to be the guy on the receiving end of her attention.

After I buried my face between her legs and made her come, I helped her out of her shirt and she returned the favor, stripping me bare.

Now we're sitting together in the center of my bed. Aspen is in my lap, rubbing her tempting curves all over me, and I have no idea how I got so fortunate. Especially after the things I told her this morning.

God, I'm such a dick.

But she's wet and moving on top of me, and it

would be easy to change our angle and bury myself inside her. But I need to get a condom, and the last thing I want to do after my massive failure is rush her. Even if I am about to explode.

Her mouth lingers on mine, and when we part, she gives me a shy look. Without a word about what she's planning, she climbs from my lap and stands next to the bed. Then she pats one of my thighs until I swing my legs over the edge of the bed, resting my feet on the floor. She sinks to her knees between my parted thighs and brings one hand to my rigid cock. A slow exhale pushes past my lips.

Her gaze mischievously meets mine while her fingers trace the length of my shaft in her palm. A shudder runs through me. Aspen pumps me in her fist and lowers her head to take me in the warmth of her mouth. I take a slow, deep breath, trying to get myself in check.

Oh.

Shit.

Can't.

Think.

Straight.

Uh.

I cup her jaw in one hand as her sweet lips move slowly up and down over me. As if to tease me. As if to draw out my pleasure. But then she begins moving over me in hot, steady strokes, sliding her fist along with her mouth.

"Yes, sweetheart. *Fuck*. Your mouth is perfect." I groan as pleasure crashes over me.

Over the last few months, I've convinced myself I'm not built for this. This level of intimacy and comfort, or tender care from a good woman. I told myself that drunken hookups in the back corners of bars were all I deserved after breaking my ex's heart. I'm a bad guy. Not someone who should be adored with worshipful gazes or soft touches.

But Aspen, it seems, never got that memo. She touches me with reverence and so much tenderness that my heart nearly bursts.

She's dropped to her knees and is sucking on my cock like I'm her boyfriend and this isn't all just pretend. She swallows me while I touch her hair and rub her shoulder, and I almost die of happiness at how fucking good it feels to be taken care of this way.

Those blue eyes meet mine, and whatever control I have left vanishes. I stroke the silky length of her hair, my hips lifting up from the bed, even though I tell them not to.

Slow down.

Let her set the pace.

It doesn't work. I'm way too close.

"Aspen. *Fuck.*" I groan and touch her cheek. "Gonna come. Better stop if you don't want that."

It's not the most romantic thing I've ever said, but those words seem to get her attention. With one last seductive kiss to the swollen head of my cock, she grins and rises to her feet.

Hell, she's hot. I fight to catch my breath while my heart beats wildly.

"Do you have more condoms?"

Wolfishly, I grin. "Stay put." Ducking into the hall, I retrieve a fistful of condoms from Saint's stash in his closet and toss them onto the nightstand as Aspen laughs.

"Someone's ambitious."

I smirk. "No, I don't expect anything. You know that. Everything we do from here on out is your call. Hell, it's always been your call, now that I think about it."

She likes this. Leaning down to kiss me in a

tender way, she pats my chest. "Lie down."

I obey as she selects a condom and hands me the package.

It's all the reassurance I need. I ready myself for her as she climbs on board, straddling my thighs. While I lift on one elbow to reach her lips, she touches my jaw and sinks onto my cock so slowly that my lungs seize.

I can't breathe.

Can't think.

Can't do anything but lie here at her mercy and let her fuck me. She's running the show now, and the pace she sets is leisurely. Unhurried. Like we have all night to pleasure each other. And I guess we do, which is the best thought ever.

"So good." I groan again, bringing my hands to her breasts to tease her nipples, and Aspen gasps. "Love the way you look riding me."

She moves faster now, finding a spot that makes her shiver in my arms.

"That's it," I encourage her.

I fill my hands with her ass as she rocks over me. It's perfect.

Aspen watches me, but she's quiet. And though

her features are painted in bliss, I'm dying to know what she's thinking.

"Feel good?" I murmur.

She presses one hand over my heart and nods. "Too good."

Her words are like a shot straight through me.

It doesn't take long until she's coming undone, trembling and moaning something that sounds a lot like my name.

The heat of Aspen's body clutching at mine causes me to lose the reins on my careful control. I grip her waist and my hips lift in erratic bursts, meeting her with firm thrusts. She collapses on top of me—chest to chest, her heart pounding—as I fill the condom with a release so powerful, every muscle in my body locks up at once.

That's when I know that I'm officially done for.

16

ASPEN

The brewery is busy this afternoon, its tables and booths packed full of locals watching the Toronto Bluejays game.

"Do you want to go somewhere else?" Alex has to lean in close so I can hear him over the cheering, his lips brushing against my ear.

A hot, liquid feeling shoots down my spine, and I press into his side to return the favor. "No, I like this place. Let's stay."

If I were alone, I might duck out and try to find a less crowded spot where I don't run the risk of being elbowed in the face. But Alex guards me with his burly body, one arm wrapped around my waist, and the other shouldering aside distracted fans. He maneuvers us through the crowd until we find two open seats at the end of a communal table.

Miraculously, one of the waitstaff finds us and takes our order—two fruity IPAs, and a plate of specialty brisket tacos to share.

Spending the afternoon in town has proven to be the perfect cure for cabin fever. If we stayed at the cabin any longer, I was starting to think we'd never get out of bed. Not that I'm against that scenario, mind you.

"We're going to be regulars soon enough," I say, joking as the server disappears to put in our orders.

Alex counts on one hand, pretending to do a really difficult math problem. "I don't think our combined total of three visits makes us regulars."

"Let a girl dream." I pout, pushing out my lower lip and batting my eyelashes. Darkening by the second, his eyes are trained on my mouth. I wore lipstick tonight, a smoky nude that I save for special occasions.

Alex smiles. "I'm all for dreams. Do you want to live in a town like this someday?"

"An idyllic little safe haven about a yard's throw from the prettiest lake I've ever seen? Nah. Sounds awful." I wink at him, enjoying the way his smile grows. It's another non-date, sure, but that doesn't mean I won't shamelessly flirt with the man. Especially after I know what he can do between the sheets.

After the server returns with our food and drinks, I lean over the table to grab my share, giving Alex an eyeful of cleavage. Once he's done taking in the view, he blinks up at me, watching the first bite disappear behind my lips.

"Unrelated, but you look beautiful tonight," Alex says nonchalantly.

My cheeks turn hot. *That's not fair.*

"Thanks," I murmur into my beer. "Gotta try a little harder when I'm going out in public with a face like yours."

Alex rolls his eyes but smiles. "We've got about twenty minutes before the movie starts."

I could swear his cheekbones redden just a teensy bit. Making Alex Braun blush? Way too fun.

We dig into our food, making good time. It's not strictly "dinner and a movie," but it certainly feels like that kind of night. While Alex settles the bill, I mentally count how many times I've grabbed dinner with a friend before seeing a movie. Plenty of times. Did we usually split the bill? Well, yes.

Alex takes my hand and leads me out the door wearing a contagious smile. I can't help but think that he's unlike any friend I've ever had. He's a guy, for one. A guy I'm currently having top-of-the-line sex with.

I've never been in a friends-with-benefits situation before. The movies I've seen usually end with the characters catching feelings and finding their happily-ever-after together. In real life, with a public figure, no less, I'm playing a dangerous game.

I have feelings—all *sorts* of feelings. I just can't tell where they start . . . my libido or my heart?

We find the theater with a few minutes left to spare. It's a historical building, with old movie posters lining the paneled walls and soft jazz playing in the background. Alex pays for the tickets, and even though we're both pretty stuffed, I still buy us a large bag of popcorn to share. It takes some convincing before Alex pockets his wallet.

It's not a date if I don't let him pay for *everything*, right?

The movie Alex chose for us is a black-and-white monster flick from the fifties. When the monster's first victim is dragged off into the steaming swamp to die offscreen, I can't help but break into a fit of giggles. And with Alex whispering in my ear the whole time, the laughter doesn't stop until long after the credits roll.

"It would take hours, you know, just to get in costume," I say as we walk back to the car. "They didn't have the option of CGI, so you can only imagine how heavy all the gear was. I'm convinced the 'monster walk' originated just because it was impossible to walk normally with all that crap on."

"You know a lot about old movies." Alex chuckles, opening the car door for me.

"My dad was a film buff." I grin, proud of the nerd I am. "He taught me everything he knew."

Alex nods, squeezing my shoulder with a kind look in his eye.

I never in a million years thought I'd be comfortable enough with someone to share such personal details about my life. I could never talk to my ex about my dad, besides the one time I briefly explained why he isn't around anymore. Dale always changed the subject if I reminisced, so eventually I learned to keep my memories bottled up, because why share them with someone who didn't respect my dad's memory?

But Alex brings out the vulnerability in me. Better yet, he actually listens and wants to know.

On the car ride back to the cabin, we swap stories about our childhoods. To my surprise, Alex admits that he didn't start playing hockey until middle school.

"My mom thought it was too violent. I argued that it doesn't really get bloody until you're in the big leagues, which didn't help. She finally let me try out for the team when I was in seventh grade."

"I hope she's supportive now." I giggle, because it's absurd to think that this mountain of muscle almost didn't play the sport that's earned him millions, all because his mom said no. It's kind of sweet, actually.

"Oh, she still thinks it's too violent." He smirks. "But she definitely sees the value now that the family's debt-free."

I'm suddenly reminded of the time at the store with the man who couldn't afford groceries for his family. How Alex came to the rescue and paid the bill, no questions asked. "You're a very generous man, Alex Braun."

There's that hint of color brightening his cheekbones again. Like I said, *way* too fun.

Finally, he says, "In a world like this, someone has to be."

I snag one of his hands from the steering wheel and give it a squeeze. For the rest of the ride, we hold hands in comfortable silence.

When we pull into the drive, Alex stiffens. "Did you leave any lights on?" he asks, his voice more serious than it's been all night. The cabin practically glows, all the windows lit up.

What the . . .

"I . . . no, I don't think so. But I know I definitely locked up." I swallow, my anxiety mounting.

Did someone break in while we were in town? Is Saint here? Suddenly, our summer of fun is at the mercy of being snatched away from us.

It's then that I notice the silver pickup truck parked at the side of the house.

"Stay here. Keep the car running." Alex's arms flex as he grips the steering wheel. He's in full-on protector mode now, watching the house for signs of danger. He gets out of the car and stalks up the driveway toward the front door.

"Anyone in there?" he calls out with a hard edge in his voice. If I were a burglar, I'd be running for the hills already.

In a bizarre turn of events, an older woman wearing glasses peeks out the front door with a look of interest. "Oh, hello. Are you the caretaker?"

"Yes," I yell, leaning out the car window. Who the heck is this woman?

To make matters even stranger, an older gentleman pops his head out the door too. "Have we got guests, Cindy?"

"I think we're the guests, Burt." Cindy laughs, approaching Alex with an outstretched hand. "Lucinda St. James. I take it you're friends with our Price?"

Price? No one calls him Price. It's then that I realize these are Saint's parents. He mentioned in his email that his mom and dad like to stop by the cabin every now and then. Relieved, I reach over to turn off the car and then join Alex, who is visibly more relaxed.

"I'm Alex, and this is Aspen. We've been taking care of the place for the past few weeks."

"I hope we didn't spook ya." Burt chortles, placing a hand on his wife's shoulder. "We tried calling the house, but no one picked up. Price gave us your cell number, Aspen, but we couldn't get through. Service can be so darn spotty up here. Come on in."

We follow the couple inside, sharing a bewildered look behind their backs. I pull Alex in to whisper in his ear, "Don't think I missed your sexy little white knight moment."

Alex chuckles, low in his chest. "You thought

that was sexy?"

"Mm-hmm. I'll have to tell you all about it later tonight."

He growls in approval, giving my ass cheek a quick squeeze before the couple turns around.

Burt tells us that they live about an hour's drive from the cabin. "We were passing through on our way home from town and decided to stop by. Hope that's all right. Looks fantastic in there, by the way."

"Of course. I mean, this is your son's cabin," I say, suddenly feeling put on the spot. I'm nearly done with the larger tasks on my list, but there's definitely work left to do.

"Aspen, you've done a wonderful job with the place." Cindy pats my arm excitedly. "Price has owned this cabin for years, and it's never looked this nice. I thought it was destined to be a dusty bachelor pad forever."

"It's hard work," I say with a smile, "but I've really enjoyed it."

"Braun, right?" Burt shakes Alex's hand with a firm grip. "I was just firing up the grill. I brought enough beef for all of us to have burgers—really good stuff too. I get it from a local butcher who does his business with farms only a couple hundred miles south of us."

Burt rambles on, leading Alex out the sliding doors and onto the deck. Alex shoots me a wide-eyed look that would make me keel over laughing if I weren't entertaining my own new friend.

"Now tell me," Cindy says with a glint in her eye. "I'm not too familiar with the team these days. It's always changing. Does your beau play hockey too?"

"Oh, n-no, we're not together. We're just friends," I stutter, the room feeling ten times warmer. "But, um, yeah, Alex plays for the Boston Titans with Saint."

I follow her into the kitchen, joining her at the island where she finishes slicing a pineapple. The air is fragrant with the smell of apples, grapes, bananas, kiwis, and . . . something sharp. I spot an open bottle of vodka on the counter.

"Want some, dear?" she asks, already mixing me a glass. "I make a mean Cape Cod."

"Definitely," I say with a grin, bellying up to the island to pick up where she left off with the pineapple. "What's all the fruit for?"

"A simple fruit salad," she says before shooting me a wink. "Family recipe. Burt's got a bit of a sweet tooth."

"Me too," I say, my mouth watering. Brisket tacos, beer, popcorn, and now a delicious homemade meal? Second only to my birthday, this day has really pampered me.

"Too bad the two of you aren't dating. You'd be such a stunning couple." Cindy sighs, nodding toward the men outside.

Alex throws his head back in laughter, clapping Burt on the shoulder like they're old friends.

In a moment of weakness, I let myself imagine Alex meeting my dad. The easy conversation, the inside jokes. Would they have been fast friends too? I'll bet they would have. My heart aches at the thought of what will never be.

Cindy must catch my expression, because she says, "Oh dear. It's complicated, isn't it?"

I shake off my sadness and give her a half smile. "Yes, in more ways than one." I catch Alex's eyes through the glass, and a warm feeling blossoms in my chest when he tilts his head just so, his smile sweeter than any fruit.

Cindy bumps me with her hip. "Burt used to look at me like that when we were 'just friends' too."

I laugh. "Did he? What changed?"

"Oh, you know. These things have a strange way of working themselves out. And if it stays complicated, I know for a fact that my son is single."

I chuckle under my breath. *Single* is the G-rated word for Saint's R-rated lifestyle. But I wouldn't dare tell his mom that. She may already know. The humorous sparkle in her eyes reminds me of the team's trademark playboy. The apple doesn't fall far from the tree, as they say.

"Voilà." Cindy drops a handful of candied cranberries in my drink with a flourish before putting it in my hands. "Enjoy."

I thank her and take a sip, enjoying the tart sweetness of it.

Dinner is delightful. It's a bit of a challenge to keep up with the conversation, seeing as I've only really talked to one person for the past few weeks. And the drinks are strong, a lot stronger than they seem. When I switch to water, Alex gives me an understanding look and carries the brunt of the conversation from there.

He's a hit with Cindy and Burt. I mean, look at

him. How could you not be absolutely smitten? His dark hair is messy, and there's a few days' worth of stubble on his jaw. His eyes flicker with mischief in the low light, and he laughs easily and often. I love just looking at him.

When our late dinner is done and the evening winds down, Cindy and Burt say their good-byes, leaving with promises to connect with us when they come to Boston for the next home game.

I'm a little sad to see them go, but it's been a long day and I'm ready for bed. Alex closes the front door when their taillights disappear around the bend.

"You tired?" he asks, wrapping one arm around me to pull me into his chest.

He's so warm and solid. I wish I could fall asleep right here and now. I have a vague memory of something I said earlier . . . something about how sexy Alex's bodyguard routine was? Of telling him all about it in the bedroom tonight? But even as I entertain the thought of sex, I yawn.

"Yeah." I sigh, nuzzling my nose against his shirt. "Did you have a nice time?"

"Actually, I did." He chuckles, and the sound vibrates pleasantly against my cheek. "When we were grilling, Burt told me all his hockey predictions for the year."

"Oh yeah?"

"Says I need to watch my angles. And that if I keep on the straight and narrow, I could make all the difference for the team this year."

I slowly lift my chin and meet his eyes. What does the straight and narrow look like for Alex? Does he see me at his side in that scenario?

I have so many questions, but all I do is give him a soft, encouraging smile. "I believe that too."

Alex kisses me on the forehead, a gesture far too intimate for friends with benefits. I wrap my arms around him and bury my face in his chest again.

Maybe if I don't let go, things don't have to change between us. Maybe the looming season can wait a little longer, and the world can remain just me and Alex.

17

ASPEN

Rain plinks against the cabin's windows in a gloomy onslaught. It started sprinkling around four o'clock while I was weeding the front flower beds and hasn't let up since. Now the storm seems to be intensifying. As I'm cleaning the last of dinner from my plate, a boom of thunder makes me shiver.

"It's getting worse," I say, wrapping my arms around myself. I think about hurrying upstairs to grab a sweater, but Alex cuts in with a much better idea.

"How about I start a fire?" He reaches for me, running a warm, calloused hand up and down my arm.

The touch thaws me a bit but does nothing to chase away the goose bumps. I don't know if I'll ever get used to the feel of his big, masculine hands on my bare skin.

"That sounds perfect."

While Alex gets to work in the living room, I take it upon myself to empty and reload the dishwasher. It occurs to me that I know precisely where every glass, dish, and utensil go, like I've lived in this place my whole life. A lump forms in my throat at the realization that I've only got a couple more weeks left under this roof.

More importantly, I only have a few more weeks left with Alex.

I press the WASH button and listen to the gentle hum of the dishwasher as the water starts to flow. I need a drink. When I raid the pantry for something sweet, my gaze lands on a package of hot chocolate mix. Pair that with a splash of peppermint liqueur? Heaven.

Alex lays out a couple of heavy blankets in front of the growing fire as I join him. I offer him a brimming mug of steaming hot chocolate with a sly smile.

"What's this?" he asks, moving his long legs to make room for me on the blanket.

I settle in next to him, instantly warmed by the

fire. "Hot chocolate with a little something extra."

Giving me a skeptical look, he blows the steam off the top of his drink. I can't help but stare at his plush lips on the edge of the cup as I take a sip of my own.

When he swallows, his dark eyebrows rise in pleasant surprise. "That's good."

"Don't tell me you've never had hot chocolate with peppermint liqueur." Surprised, I shake my head in disbelief. Back in college, I would make a whole pot of it on the stove for my roommates. It's the perfect mixture of chocolatey and minty, without being too boozy.

"Can't say I have," he says with a chuckle. "But I like it."

With that, Alex sets the drink aside and leans over, pressing his beverage-warmed lips against mine. He tastes like dessert, and I can't get enough. I sigh against his mouth, enjoying how he threads one free hand through my hair, and teases my lips open with the tip of his tongue. We taste each other, slowly and sensually, without a care in the world.

But just when it seems like time has stopped, questions start racing through my mind again.

What happens when we get back to Boston?

What if we can't figure out how to just be friends, and end up treating each other like strangers? What if everything I've found in myself this summer, everything I've come to *love* about myself, fades away?

I think of my newfound sexual confidence, the desire Alex has awakened within me. I think of the way smiles come easier to me these days, now that I'm no longer burdened by a toxic partner. I think of how comforting it is to finally be accepted for who I am, instead of being criticized for who I'm not.

What if I lose all these positive changes the second I lock up the cabin for the last time?

A log in the fire snaps, and I grip the front of Alex's shirt, deepening the kiss with a throaty moan. He indulges my urgency, embracing me with equal passion. But when he pulls back, a look of concern is etched across his features.

"What is it?" He runs his fingers over the hand I've buried in his shirt, soothing me with the softest of touches. "You're shaking."

I blink and drop my chin, escaping his penetrating gaze. "Oh. I think I just got stuck in my head for a moment there."

"What were you thinking about?"

"Going home, I guess." The vaguer the better. I don't dare admit how afraid I am of losing him and the intimacy we've shared for the past few weeks. We made a deal, after all. Just for the summer.

"What about it?" Alex caresses a soft line in my cheek. "Are you worried about finding a new place?"

"Um, yeah. I guess I am." I can't unload the truth on him. Not now. Not when our whole arrangement was my idea. "I think I'm gonna have a hard time leaving here."

"I know what you mean." His gaze meets mine, and I'm pretty sure there's some hidden meaning behind those eyes of his.

I snuggle against his firm chest, watching his fingers as he plays with the ends of my hair. We fall silent for a moment and listen to the crackle of the fire. After a while, my mind wanders, and I think about what a future with Alex might look like.

Would we have long, rainy nights like this, content to just rest in each other's arms? Would we weather the struggles of life together well as a couple? Especially with him traveling as much as he does during hockey season and being surrounded by countless puck bunnies?

Or would it end like it did with Dale? Like it

did with Eden?

"You wanna know something?" Alex asks suddenly, pulling me out of my spiral and back down to planet Earth.

"Yes, of course." I caress his forearm with my fingertips.

"This has probably been the best summer of my life."

My hand stills on his skin. *Is he screwing with me?*

I pull back to look him in the eye, but his expression is open and honest, reflecting the warmth of the fire. "Why do you say that?"

Alex shrugs, lifting a strand of my pale hair and rubbing it between his fingertips. "I haven't always felt like I could be myself, you know? Back home, it's like everyone has already decided who I am. But here with you, I can be the kind of man I want to be." He pauses, a thoughtful look in his eye. "I suppose there's something centering about being out in the middle of nowhere with nothing but a beautiful woman to distract you."

I blush, pushing his shoulder playfully. "Charmer."

"I mean it, though," he says with a roguish

smirk, but there's something insistent in his voice. "This summer could have been hella awkward. Or at best, boring. But it wasn't, because you didn't dismiss me as some asshole you had to keep tabs on from a distance. For the first time in a long time, I wasn't seen as a time bomb. I got to be a person. I got to be just Alex. And I—" He starts to say something but seems to think better of it before settling on, "I'm glad it all turned out the way it did."

"Me too," I murmur, searching his eyes for answers to questions I'm not brave enough to ask.

Alex threads his fingers through mine. "You okay?"

"Yeah," I manage to say, trying to convince myself that it's not a lie. "It's been strange, imagining going back to Boston. Back to the way things were. I get what you mean, about feeling like yourself here. I feel that way too. And I like this version of Aspen the best."

"I do too," he says quietly, and I lock eyes with him, a little surprised. "Sorry. I didn't mean to interrupt. Continue."

And this Aspen really, really likes you.

It would be so easy to say those words right now, bundled up next to the fire with the warmth of hot chocolate and liqueur buzzing in my veins. But

I can't risk the possibility of rejection, not so soon in my recovery from my last mess of a relationship. My heart couldn't take it.

So instead, I say, "I guess I've been really spoiled this summer. I mean, for starters, whatever apartment I find isn't going to come close to being this nice." I gesture around us halfheartedly.

"You'll find a place. It might not have a hot tub and be on a lake, but it'll be right for you." Alex nudges my arm with a wink.

A grin creeps across my lips, eager to replace my frown. I don't want to waste any more precious time being worried.

"No hot tub?" I pout. "What about a fireplace?"

"Is that a requirement?"

"Oh yeah." I giggle. "Fireplaces are perfect for cozying up in front of." I nuzzle his neck, trailing kisses along the corded muscle there.

Alex exhales deeply, leaning into my touch. "Hmm? All by yourself?" he asks, his voice huskier now.

I shiver as he trails one hand up my thigh to the edge of my shirt, tugging the fabric away to caress more of my skin.

"No," I whisper, gasping when his thumb brushes the underside of my breast. "With . . . a book."

"A book? Not a man?"

Both of his hands are under my shirt now, his fingers drawing teasing circles around my nipples before pinching them experimentally. I arch my back, and Alex takes the opportunity to lift off my shirt and palm my exposed chest. I pull his face to mine and kiss him deeply. When we part, it's with gasping breaths.

His eyes are dark with desire. The time for words is done.

Alex leans back only far enough to pull off his shirt. I rake my fingers against the hard ridges of his abs, enjoying how they flex against my touch. Gripping my leg, he pushes us down into the blanket, lining his cock—already hard and eager—up with my achingly wet core. He grinds against me, watching my face closely as I moan.

I lift my hips off the blanket as an invitation.

He takes the hint and tugs my shorts and panties down my legs, brushing my skin with lazy, unhurried kisses on the way down. Then he unbuttons his own pants and pulls them down his long, athletic legs, but not before grabbing a condom from his back pocket.

Soon, there's nothing between us. Only hot, magnetic skin on skin, and more desire than I've ever felt.

Alex lowers his hand between my legs, feeling exactly how ready I am. With his other hand, he unrolls a condom down the length of his erection, all the while staring intently at my eyes, my lips, my breasts. Just the heat of his gaze is enough to make my pulse quicken. Then he teases my opening with the tip, not quite entering me. I moan, so close to losing my mind.

"What do you want, Aspen?" His voice is warm and tender, like all he cares about in this moment is me.

I dig my fingernails into his lower back, any semblance of control long gone now that I'm sprawled naked beneath him. Gasping, I say, "I want you inside me."

He wraps his hands around my hips, the press of his fingers electrifying. With one gentle push, Alex fills me. My toes curl as he drives himself deep inside me, every last inch of him buried in my core. When he doesn't move, I prompt him with my hips, a desperate whimper escaping my lips. He smirks, leaning over to kiss me lightly before he starts to move his hips in slow, even strokes.

"Oh, baby," he says softly. "I just want you to feel good."

"You . . . you feel amazing," I say on a groan.

It's barely been two minutes since we began, and I'm already coming apart at the seams. I rock my hips in rhythm with him, moaning when he hits that incredible place deep inside me. He finds my clit with his thumb, circling it with a featherlight pressure that has me quivering. It feels like the flames have leaped from the fireplace and are licking their way up my arms and legs, promising to consume me whole.

"Alex . . ."

His name trembles on my lips as I come, my body rocking against his in endless pleasure. I hold on to him as he fucks me through my orgasm, drawing out my pleasure until I can't see anything but him.

With a strangled groan, Alex buries himself deep and shudders. "*Fuck*. Can't last with you."

I press my lips to his throat, tasting his stubbled skin as he groans again. With another deep thrust, he follows my lead off the edge into his own release.

It takes us a while to catch our breath. When we do, Alex presses a soft kiss to my cheek and reluctantly gets up to discard the condom. Joining me on the blanket again, he pulls me into his arms, and I gladly let him wrap me up against his chest.

Tears prick at the corners of my eyes when I realize that I've never felt safer. I have to swallow those tears away when I realize that this feeling won't last.

"Can we sleep here? Just for a little while?" I mumble, my lips brushing lazily against his bicep.

"Whatever you want." He sighs into my neck, dragging a blanket from the couch over our naked bodies.

With the steady rainfall and crackling fire creating a soothing white noise, I savor the sound of Alex's soft breaths slowing as he's lulled to relaxation. And even though nothing between us is certain, it's somehow still perfect.

18

ALEX

"That's it. Just like that," I call out to the group of kids I've been assigned to work with. There are a dozen of them, and each one is a fantastic skater.

When I was their age, I had promise and lots of potential, but I wasn't this skilled. Not by a long shot. I arrived here two hours ago, and after playing a memory game to learn their names, which was mostly for my benefit since I had no hope of remembering them, we've taken to the ice.

"Do it again . . . um . . . *you*," I call out, pointing to the tall, lanky kid at center ice.

Too bad I just now realized that all ten-year-old boys look the same wearing full hockey gear that includes a face cage. One of the other coaches has added a strip of tape to each of the helmets of the kids in his group with their first names. *Smart.* If I do this camp again next year, I'm going to steal that hack and bring a roll of duct tape with me.

I had them start with the basics so I could assess their skill level. Forward and backward sizzles. Hockey stops. C-cuts and backward crossovers. But we quickly moved on to stick handling and passing drills. And after lunch, I think we'll have a scrimmage. I'm actually having way more fun than I thought I would.

When I left Aspen yesterday to make the five-hour drive down here to New York, I was regretting that I'd even volunteered to do this. Because leaving the cozy situationship she and I have been sharing this summer . . . ten out of ten, do not recommend. Spending even one night away from her when we have so little time left is tricky.

Still, it feels good to be on the ice. Even if I've never been to this city, never stepped foot inside this facility before, as soon as my skates hit the ice, it felt like coming home. And it feels good to give back to the next generation of hockey players. Plus, if that sexual harassment story breaks, I'll need every last bit of goodwill I can muster. It's not something I want to think about right now, though.

We take a break for lunch, and then after, I lace up my skates, joining the boys on the ice for an action-packed scrimmage. We're not playing with goalies, but I secretly love the fact that the quietest kid in my group has taken it upon himself to guard our net—like he knows this isn't *really* a competition without some healthy defense of our goal.

A kid after my own heart.

When the kids finish on the ice, I push myself through some drills, pumping my legs until I'm racing across the rink, taking the corners like I'm chasing an opponent. I hear cheers and whistles as I pass the kids. They might think I'm doing this to entertain them with my speed and power, but really, I'm all too aware of how very little ice time I've gotten this summer. Twenty minutes later, my heart rate is up and I'm drenched in sweat.

At the end of the day, I change in the locker room and head out, opting to shower in my hotel room before I go and meet Jaxon and Nelle for dinner.

Since I have a few minutes before I need to leave, I grab my phone and text Aspen.

How's everything going?

I throw on a clean T-shirt while I wait for her to reply.

Hey. Just fine. I found a paddleboard in the shed, so I gave it a try today.

Yeah? **I type back.** Sounds like fun.

It wasn't. Total disaster. **She adds a crying emoji face.**

Uh-oh. I wonder what happened, but I don't have to wait long, because Aspen's next message appears.

I got to experience that freezing cold water again.

Fun, **I type back with a chuckle.**

How's hockey camp? **she replies.**

Good. I'm done for the day. Going to meet my sister and nephew now.

Have fun!

Will do, **I text her. Then I pocket my phone and gather up my keys and wallet.**

I can't help but think how easy it is with Aspen.

• • •

"Uncle Alex," Jaxon calls out when he spots me.

We decided to meet at a go-kart track near my hotel, and I've just parked my car when I spot them on the sidewalk near the entrance. I jog the last few paces and lift my nephew into my arms.

Surprised, I say, "You got taller."

"Yup," he says proudly.

I greet Nelle with a kiss on her cheek.

"You look well," she says, giving my shoulder a playful punch.

"Thanks. So do you. How's life?"

Nelle fills me in on the latest drama with the teachers union she's a member of as I lead them both inside, where we grab a table and purchase some tickets for the arcade. Then Jaxon disappears into a maze of arcade games, and we follow, Nelle watching him closely.

We stand back while Jaxon feeds a ticket into a game of Skee-Ball and begins tossing the balls at the target.

"How's your summer been?" Nelle says, straightening the bill of my baseball cap. "Staying out of trouble?"

"Yes, *Mom*." I roll my eyes. "It's been really chill. I've actually been hanging out with a girl named Aspen."

Nelle's smile widens. "That's *interesting*. Is she similar to Eden?"

I snort. Aspen is basically Eden's complete opposite. "Not at all."

Eden had trouble giving up control in most things. She had a spreadsheet for every occasion. Even letting me cook was like some big ordeal. I didn't chop the tomatoes the way she liked, or my garlic wasn't minced fine enough. Whereas Aspen just lets me do my thing and appreciates it.

"Maybe that's a good thing," Nelle says, making a pleased sound, but I don't respond.

I have no idea what the hell I was thinking telling Nelle about Aspen. Aspen and I are a very temporary thing. Someone fun to distract myself with this summer. And Nelle isn't likely to forget that I brought her up. With my luck, she'll be asking me about bringing Aspen home for Christmas. And by Christmas, we'll be long over. We'll be back to hockey player and assistant.

What was I thinking even bringing her up?

"It's not a big deal," I say. "She's just a friend."

Nelle's expression softens, her smile growing. "Okay. If you say so."

"I'm serious, Nelle." My tone holds a warning, but my sister just smiles. "Don't think too much into it."

I don't bother explaining that Aspen and I are both coming off breakups, and that this is a rebound. I'm pretty sure there's a law against nature about explaining to your sibling that Aspen and I have mutually agreed to blow off steam by hooking up this summer.

The only reason I brought it up is because I'd feel weird not telling anyone about Aspen. She's who I've been spending all my time with, after all.

"Let's go drive some go-karts before we have dinner. You game?" I ask.

Nelle calls out to Jaxon, and he leads the way.

After a couple of laps around the track and a slice of pizza, Jaxon finishes his game and jogs over to where we're standing by the windows. "I lost. Twice," he says glumly.

"You know how many times I've lost in my

life?"

He shakes his head.

"Lots." I hoist him up onto my shoulders. "So, don't sweat it, kid. Losing makes you hungry."

"But we just ate," he says in protest.

I chuckle. "Not hungry for *food*, little man. Hungry for *more*, for competition. Hungry to improve. And win."

"Oh," Jaxon says in a knowing tone.

Nelle gives me a look. "We'd better get going." She's always been pretty strict, and I have a feeling by the time they make the drive home, it'll be long past Jaxon's bedtime.

I walk them out into the parking lot and over to where Nelle's parked. "Pick out the SUV you want, and text me," I tell her.

She rolls her eyes. "The van's still got some life in it."

"Not for you, it doesn't. I'm buying you the SUV." Last Thanksgiving, she admitted to me she liked the look of the new SUV model when I pestered her about the minivan starting to show its age.

"You want the one with the built-in screens to watch movies, right, Jax?" I say, setting him on his feet beside the minivan, and he cheers.

"Yeah!"

Nelle rolls her eyes. "It's just an added expense. And believe me, he gets plenty of screen time."

"It'd be a good feature to have for road trips. Like when you guys drive up to Boston and see me. Right, little man?"

"Can you get us tickets to a game, Uncle Alex?"

"Of course I can." I ruffle his hair. "I'll even get you into the dressing room to meet the guys."

"Thanks for tonight," Nelle says. "Stay out of trouble, okay?"

"I'll do that."

"Oh, and Alex? Say hi to Aspen for me."

Shit.

• • •

The following day flies by coaching ten-year-olds on the ice. We have a short ceremony at the end, where each kid is presented with a puck signed by me and a certificate of completion.

Tonight, I have plans to grab an early dinner

with the other coaches, but first I check my phone to see if Aspen messaged me. There's nothing from her, but a message from Tate, the Titans rookie, pops up instead. He joined the team last year. I haven't hung out with him much, but he seems cool.

Where have you been hiding this summer, big guy?

Canada.

No shit? Me too. Come over and visit anytime.

Canada is a big country, moron, **I type back, chuckling.**

Ha. True, **he texts back.**

I'm crashing at Saint's place in Ottawa. You?

Hiking in Vancouver. This place is sick.

Nice. Just you?

Yup, all by my lonesome. Just wanted to say don't be a stranger. We're gonna kill it this season.

Hell yeah, we are. **I grin at his enthusiasm. Oh, to be young and optimistic again.**

I'm going to make that points differential my bitch.

I laugh. You do that, rookie.

He texts back a thumbs-up emoji. **See you at training camp.**

See you then.

I consider texting Aspen next, maybe to ask her how she's faring without me. Some taunt perhaps about what she's doing for dinner without her personal chef. But when I look at the time, I realize I really do need to get going. I don't want to be late meeting the other coaches.

I stuff my phone in my pocket and head out to the local barbecue restaurant where we agreed to meet. While the rest of the guys order beer, I stick to water because Tate was right. Soon, I'll be at training camp, and it will become glaringly obvious who spent the summer drinking beer and who spent the summer training.

While I'm at dinner, my lawyer, Hugh, leaves a voice mail, but I'm in no mood to listen to it.

After I pick up the check for dinner, there's some bro-hugs and handshakes, and then I'm alone in my car, driving back to the hotel. I'm scheduled to stay another night and drive out in the morning, but I realize that if I leave now, I could make it back to the cabin by midnight. And I'd much rather sleep with Aspen tonight than alone in the hard hotel bed. With that decision made, I rush back to the hotel, pack my bags, and check out early.

• • •

When I make it back to the lake house just before midnight, I see that the porch light's been left on.

I considered surprising Aspen, but then I realized arriving after dark would probably scare the hell out of her. I didn't want her to think someone was breaking in and panic. So I called her from the road and told her I was on my way. That was around nine, and she was already yawning.

"Don't wait up," I told her, but I secretly hoped

that she would. But the house is dark and completely quiet when I let myself inside.

I find her in my bed, curled up onto her side. Her head lifts from the pillow as I step inside the room. We've been sleeping in her room, so I'm a little surprised to find her here.

"Hey," I whisper. "Didn't mean to wake you."

Wordlessly, she reaches one hand toward me. With a grin, I strip down to my boxers and climb in behind her, pulling her into my chest. Aspen makes a sleepy, satisfied sound and relaxes, her soft curves pressing against me.

Man, it feels good to just hold her. I need to brush my teeth. And plug in my phone. But I'm way too comfortable to move.

And knowing how few nights we have left . . . I stay put and just enjoy holding Aspen.

19

ASPEN

I wake up still wrapped in Alex's arms, and a smile spreads across my lips before I even open my eyes. I curled up in his bed last night, even though we've mostly been sleeping in mine. This bed smelled like him, so I climbed in to await his return.

While he was away, I thought of nothing but him. I thought about the first time we had sex, and how the morning after he tried to push me away. It hurt. And maybe it shouldn't, but it actually endeared me to him even more. Alex tried to do the right thing and put the brakes on our attraction as it skidded out of control. Tried to give me an out, or at least time to think.

But all I did with that time was think about how much I wanted him. His scorching-hot kisses and his strong arms wrapped around me. His sweet gesture with the hot tub sealed the deal. I all but pounced on him that very same night.

To be honest, this summer has been everything I could have dreamed of and more. It feels cliché to admit, but I really did need to get lost in the Canadian wilderness in order to find myself. Leaving the cabin is going to be a lot harder than I ever could have anticipated when I took the job. Who would have known that I'd grow so attached to the place? Not to mention the man who came with it . . .

Alex was only gone for two nights, but being alone in the middle of the wilderness seemed to make the hours tick by more slowly. I've missed him, and while I can't admit that with words without inviting all kinds of intrusive questions that I'm not ready to answer, I can *show* him.

Turning in his arms to face him, I'm surprised to see Alex is already awake, a sleepy smile on his full mouth. "Morning." I press a kiss to his throat.

"Morning."

"Been up long?"

"Not long," he says, running his fingers through my hair. "Just a few minutes."

I nestle into the broad expanse of his chest and let out a happy sigh. "Let's stay in bed all day."

Alex chuckles. "I'm good with that plan. But . . ."

I groan. "Why does there have to be a *but*?"

He kisses my forehead. "What about coffee?"

I concede the point, since it is a very valid one. "Okay. But can we drink it in bed?"

"Absolutely. Give me five minutes. Six, tops."

He rises from the bed dressed only in his black boxer briefs and disappears into the hallway, while I lift on one elbow to watch his sexy retreat.

Deciding a quick trip to the bathroom is in order, I climb out of bed reluctantly. After getting my hair and morning breath under control, I slip under the heavy duvet again.

A minute later, Alex returns with two steaming mugs of coffee. "Here you go."

He hands one of the mugs to me, and I take a small sip. It's delicious.

It's going to be hard going back to the real world. No one to make me coffee or cook for me. No muscular, hunky hockey player to share my bed.

Don't think about it.

Not yet.

Alex settles in beside me, quietly sipping his coffee. I lean back against him, happy to use his shoulder as my pillow. I ask a few questions, and he fills me in on his trip to New York and his time spent with his sister and nephew.

I don't want to admit it to him, but part of me has wondered if he'd just decide to stay in the States. Maybe getting back in the hockey scene would have made him homesick for hockey or his teammates. I even braced myself for a phone call saying he wasn't coming back. Instead, we kept in touch, texting throughout the days about inconsequential things. Mostly, he teased me about my inability to feed myself. It was cute.

"We could make a bonfire tonight," he says. "And maybe even go fishing. Catch ourselves something for dinner."

I smile at the idea of that. "I'm game."

When I set my coffee mug on the nightstand, a bottle of lubricant catches my attention. It's a small bottle—half-full—unscented. It isn't something we've used together.

I pick it up and lift one eyebrow in his direction. "You use this?"

Alex chuckles. "Uh, yeah, to jerk off." He's certainly not shy.

"Mmm, that's a nice thought. Could I watch?"

He sets his coffee down next to mine and faces me on the bed. "You want to watch me?"

I nod, my eager gaze locked on his. "Why not?"

He touches his lips to mine, considering this, then strokes his fingers through my hair. "Your hand would feel better than mine. But yeah. I'll show you how I like it . . . if you want."

My heart rate accelerates. "Okay." I breathe out the word as he kisses me again.

He's already half-hard, the front of his boxers tented in the sexiest way. As we lie side by side, I brush my palm against him.

He deepens our kiss with a hoarse groan and tilts my face toward his. The weight of his hand rests against my throat, his thumb right beneath my chin.

Everything about this man is so perfect, and spending time with him these last few weeks has meant everything to me. But I can't stop these intrusive thoughts about where we stand.

He was right—sex does complicate things. I have a sexy man, plans for a bonfire, and good food to look forward to later. Why can't I just be happy and enjoy it? Why do I constantly have to be thinking about what's next?

Alex's hand slides from my throat down to my chest. He pushes my tank top out of the way and fills his palm with my breast, teasing me.

"This okay?" he asks, dropping his mouth to my neck where he leaves hot, sucking kisses.

"Yeah," I murmur.

His hand moves between my legs, where he caresses me with soft touches. I arch against him and part my knees.

Oh . . . wow. I thought I was going to be the one pleasuring him, but Alex's skillful fingers are working me right toward the edge.

"Love touching you," he says, whispering the words against my parted lips.

I push my hand inside his boxers while he flips open the cap to the bottle and drizzles some lube into his palm. Then he closes his fist around his swollen shaft and begins slowly stroking himself.

It's hot as hell watching his hand move over himself . . . his muscled forearm bunching with the effort. The halted breath that shudders in his chest. As he strokes himself with one hand and me with the other, I can do little more than writhe beneath his touch.

I bring my hand to his groin and push his boxers out of the way, then trail my fingertips down until I can cup his balls in my palm.

Alex groans quietly. "That's a girl."

With a moan, I come apart, clutching his forearm between my legs and riding out the waves of pleasure. When I open my eyes, Alex is gazing down at me.

I press my mouth to his. "This was supposed to be about you."

He kisses me quickly. "Believe me, it is. It's hot as hell watching you get off."

I curl my fist around his, needing to touch him. His chest rises with a quick breath, and I can tell he's getting close.

"Ahh. *Fuck*," he mutters, his abs tightening as my hand moves along him in a quickening pace.

A few more strokes and Alex lets go, a deep groan rumbling in his chest. When his mouth finds mine, I feel the warmth of his release on my skin.

"Don't move," he says, a little breathless.

Then he moves through the bedroom, naked but completely comfortable. He returns with a soft expression and a box of tissues, which he uses to wipe the sticky globs from my stomach.

I gaze up at him adoringly while he concentrates on his task of cleaning me. But I'd give anything to know what he's thinking.

20

ASPEN

Sitting on the deck, I scroll absentmindedly through the apartment listings on my phone. Believe me, I've tried, but I can't ignore this task forever. I'm going to be back in the real world soon, and it's time I started acting like it.

A cool breeze rustles the treetops, yet another reminder that summer is on its last legs. Which means I can only enjoy the perks of freeloading at Saint's cabin for a few more days.

The apartment search was something I've been dreading ever since I packed up my old place and moved in with Eden and Holt. But there's no avoiding it now. With the extra cash I've earned from this summer gig, I might be able to afford a nice little studio after all. Or at least one that's *not* in the shady part of town.

Although, it'll never be as nice as the cabin I've been calling home. The truth is, I don't love this place for the amenities, although those are absolutely a perk. I don't even love it for the views, which are unforgettable, of course. I love this place for the memories I've created here with Alex.

But now's not the time for fantasy. It's time to be practical.

You can do this.

I sigh, making a mental note to compare the places that have utilities included in the rent. I've sent out a few inquiries and scheduled some tours for when I'm back in Boston. Luckily, there's no shortage of units available this fall, and the agents seem eager to get rid of the dead weight left from the summer. Turns out, I'm not nearly as nervous about finding a place as I am about leaving this one.

Almost as if he knows I'm thinking about him, Alex steps out onto the deck in a navy-blue hoodie, gray sweatshorts, and bare feet. His hair is still wet from his morning shower.

God, he's gorgeous. I don't think I'll ever get used to how handsome he is. He takes my breath away.

"You're up early," he says. He's carrying two cups of coffee and offers me one. Black, because he knows that's how I like it. "Thanks for getting the coffee going."

"No problem," I say with a smile. I already feel a thousand times more at ease with Alex near. "I woke up before my alarm and couldn't fall back asleep." Truth is, I barely slept at all last night.

"Hate when that happens." He heaves a sigh as he sits across from me in one of the deck chairs. "I'm gonna go into town today to grab some supplies to fix the shed. Is there anything you want me to pick up for you?"

I shrug, a proud grin spreading across my face. "Nope, because I finished the last of my to-do list yesterday."

"Well, lucky you . . . Little Miss Overachiever." Alex scowls playfully, nudging my knee with the bottom of his foot. "The shed is the last job on my list. I don't know much about replacing shingles, but I did some reading up on it last night, and it doesn't look too complicated."

As he recaps his findings, I decide to memorize this moment.

I take him in fully, from the dusting of dark hair along his muscular legs, to his flat stomach, all the way up his sculpted chest, then to his large, calloused hands casually holding his coffee mug. I commit to memory the angle of his Adam's apple, the curve of his upper lip, his dark eyelashes surrounding his strikingly blue eyes.

But it's only when I'm gazing into his eyes that a realization I should have seen coming from a mile away hits me with the force of a runaway train.

I'm in love with him.

Somewhere along the way, between the long days and even longer nights, I developed feelings for Alex. Despite my better judgment, I love him. I love his unfaltering kindness, his sense of humor, his talents in the kitchen *and* the bedroom. Not to mention those eyes and that smile.

I swallow a lump in my throat. This is not the kind of realization you want to have when faced with a deadline of returning to the real world. If I plan on telling him how I feel, I have to do it . . . like, *now.* But there's no way I'm ready for that. *Am I?*

While I debate that, my cheeks heating with my uncertainty, I realize that the new me—the post-breakup, freshly empowered Aspen—is a lot braver than I've ever been before.

I chew on my lip, running through the pros and cons in my head.

Pros? He might feel the same way, and we could start officially dating back in the city. We'd work out the complicated things (cough, cough, *Eden*), and start a life together.

Cons? My throat tightens. There are *so* many. Like, maybe he doesn't feel the same way. My confession ruins our friendship, and we never recover. I live with the shame of developing feelings for my boss's ex-boyfriend. I live with the disappointment of yet another rejection. My barely healed heart breaks into a thousand more pieces. The list goes on and on.

". . . and I'll probably swing by the brewery and pick up a six-pack of that grapefruit IPA we like."

When I resurface from my whirlpool of self-doubt, Alex is smiling at me, endearingly clueless to the earth-shattering revelation I've just had. He takes a sip of his coffee, now at a drinkable temperature. I gulp down my own, trying to swallow all the confessions threatening to escape my throat and ruin everything.

"Sounds like you've got your work cut out for you today." My voice feels tight but sounds relatively normal, given how close I am to imploding.

"How about you?"

"I've got a report to finish for Eden, so I may

get a head start on that. I may also wait until I'm back in the office and just try to enjoy these last few days before everything goes back to normal."

Alex nods in agreement. "I vote for the latter. You deserve to take some time to relax."

"You do too," I say with a soft smile. "You've got a whole season waiting for you just around the corner."

"True." He smirks into his coffee.

Ever since he got back from his trip to New York, Alex has seemed a little more excited to return to the life of a professional athlete. My own complicated feelings aside, I'm happy for him.

The question falls from my lips before I can decide what I'm really asking. "Have you given the season any thought?"

"What do you mean?"

"I mean, uh, like, how are you feeling about it all? Going back?"

Alex frowns, turning the question over in his head. "Kind of like what you said. Everything's just gonna go back to normal, right? Business as usual."

My heart clenches painfully. "And that's a

good thing?"

"Yeah. I'm actually looking forward to it."

Well, that settles it, doesn't it? There's no way this man shares the same feelings for me as I do for him. He doesn't want to rock the boat and pursue things at home with me. *Business as usual.* The last thing I want is for everything to go back to the way it was, whereas, going "back to normal" seems to be a top priority for him.

Maybe he's just talking about hockey. Maybe I'm reading into it, looking for an excuse to do the cowardly thing and protect my heart. Maybe I haven't changed as much as I thought I did.

"How about you?" Alex blinks at me, cocking his head to the side.

I don't want things to go back to normal, because "normal" means that we go back to being strangers. I don't want to lose you, Alex. I'm in love with you.

I hear the words so clearly in my head, but I can't say any of that. When I open my mouth, I'm not sure what will come out.

"Me too. Can't wait to get back into the swing of things."

I'm not sure what we talk about after that, since

all my focus is devoted to the single task of not crying.

Before he leaves to run errands in town, Alex pulls me into the kind of hug that is so comfortable and familiar, I almost lose it right then and there. I manage to pull away without letting a single tear fall, but not before memorizing the smell of him through his hoodie. Man and mint soap.

Upstairs, I watch through the bedroom window as he climbs into his car and drives out of view down the road. And that's when the dam breaks. With stinging eyes and hiccupping sobs, I let myself fall apart. I collapse onto the bed and bury my face in his pillow.

This hurts so much. Why can't he see how perfect we'd be together?

I can't let Alex see me like this. And there's no way I can endure the next few days of pretending he's just my friend-with-benefits. With no other choice but to flee, I rise to my feet and blow my nose. Then I get to work.

Tearing around the room, I toss my clothes, shoes, and toiletries into my suitcase. I know it's premature, not to mention *immature*, but every atom in my body is screaming at me to run. So I shove all traces of my summer stay into my suitcase, erasing any evidence that I was ever here at all.

I yank the festive moose ornament from its spot on my windowsill and shove it in my purse. I gather all the spa gifts Alex got me for my birthday from their spot on the floor next to the clawfoot tub. I snatch up the book I'm still reading from the living room windowsill—the book I was planning on finishing before I left the cabin. I roll up my yoga mat on the deck and tie it haphazardly to my suitcase. Each item I pack away is accompanied by a montage of memories starring the man I fell for despite all logic.

God, I'm such an idiot. He was right to push me away after that first night.

Just as I'm about to roll my suitcase out the door for the very last time, I pause.

I can't leave without any explanation. Alex will think something's happened to me, or worse, that he did something wrong. I don't want to explain to him that I couldn't cope with my unrequited feelings, but I need to leave him a note. Sniffling, I wipe my wet cheeks dry with the back of my hand.

Once I find a scrap of paper in a kitchen drawer, I settle in to write my good-bye letter—no, that's too dramatic. It's just a note, like a GONE FISHING sign or a BE BACK IN FIVE placard. Except I won't be back.

I chew on my raw lip. With an unsteady hand, I write:

Alex,

I decided to head back to Boston a few days early. I got a lead on an apartment I really like, and I want to see it in person before it gets snatched up by someone else. Just wanted you to know that I wasn't kidnapped or anything.

Thank you for your help with the cabin this summer. I'll see you when the season starts—I know it's gonna be a great one.

Aspen

I lay the pen down and turn in a slow circle, trying to memorize the place that has brought me so much peace and purpose this summer, right when I needed it the most. Wearing a smile tinged with sadness, I roll my suitcase out the cabin's front door and lock up for the last time . . . leaving a few thousand pieces of my heart inside.

21

ALEX

"You sure you don't want to come?" I asked Aspen one last time as I lingered in the kitchen before heading to town.

She shook her head, glancing at me over one shoulder. "That's okay. You go ahead. I'm going to finish a few things here and call my mom back."

I nodded. There was something different about her tone, but I let it go. "Okay. I won't be gone long. Text me if you need anything."

She nodded, and then I gave her a long hug.

I didn't want to leave—even to drive into town for shed supplies—since we were down to our final days together, but I also needed to pick up a few bottles of wine and some more condoms to replace what I'd taken from Saint. Plus, I wanted to get Aspen something special as a gift. But what to get her? A T-shirt from a gift shop doesn't exactly scream *thank you for all the tender care, all the awesome sex, all the laughs we shared this summer*.

But now when I return, the house is quiet. Wandering through each room, I look for Aspen. Not finding her inside, I head for the glass doors.

"Babe?" I call out, peeking outside onto the deck. A bird chirps back at me, but otherwise it's silent.

I take the stairs two at a time, and when I reach the master bedroom, I pause. It's empty. The bed is neatly made, and all her bags are gone. A deep, stabbing feeling radiates through my chest.

What the hell?

I never expected Aspen to be gone when I returned. She didn't say anything about taking off, but she's left, and not just to run an errand. She's gone back to Boston without saying a damn word. *Why?*

When I find a note from her downstairs on the kitchen island, I pick it up with shaking hands. After reading it twice, I'm still confused.

I thought what we shared meant something. Yeah, it was short term, but it was meaningful, wasn't it? Or was I just some rebound fling like she said she wanted at the beginning? I thought we've grown, turned into something that would transcend this place. We didn't talk about how it would work yet with my season, or with my ex being her boss, but they weren't insurmountable things. We could have figured them out. Or so I thought.

I grab my phone and consider calling her. But what will I say without sounding like an emotional mess? Or worse, a pissed-off asshole? I thought I deserved way more than just some three-line *see ya later* note, but I guess I was wrong.

Aspen's rejection feels like being punched right in the insecurities. Sure, I lost Eden, but that was my fault. I've learned a lot about myself since our breakup. I actually *am* a relationship guy. And now I know I'd like nothing more than a good woman waiting for me when I get home from away games. A woman to share home-cooked meals with me. Spending mornings laughing in bed and sleeping next to her all night, without having to worry if she was going through my phone or planning to take a selfie with me to sell to the tabloids.

But just like I always do, I managed to fuck it all up. I don't know *how*, but I know I did. Because Aspen's not here, and I'm alone.

Again.

22

ASPEN

After I insisted I could handle move-in day by myself, Eden and Holt were determined to find another way to help.

That's how I ended up with a bunch of free furnishings for my apartment, either donations from their personal collection or straight-up brand-new gifts. I squeeze against the wall on the first-floor landing so the larger of my two helpers can carry up a small but hefty table that I offhandedly said I liked when I was still staying with them.

"Thank you," I say meekly as Holt passes by me.

"You got it," he says with a nod, disappearing up the second flight of stairs and rounding the corner to enter my new apartment. It's not a big place, but a one-bedroom with central air and a combo washer-dryer unit suits me just fine.

My new full-size mattress arrived this morning, compressed into a cardboard box seemingly manageable enough for one person to move. But when I try to lift it by myself, I only end up red-faced and sore. Eden jogs down the steps, looking like an athletic-wear model with her long blond hair tied up in a high ponytail and her fit figure wrapped in comfortable but flattering workout clothes.

"Need a hand?" she asks, and I nod with a heavy sigh. Together, we lift the box up the stairs, taking breaks along the way as needed.

Propping the box against the stairway wall, I say through panting breaths, "I can't thank you enough . . . for helping me out. I just wish . . . I'd found a place that wasn't so . . . so hard to get to."

Eden waves the comment away with her hand as she sucks in a deep breath. "Don't even. It's smart to be on an upper floor. Less chance of someone breaking in through the window, you know? As a woman, I respect it."

"I hadn't thought about that." I chuckle a little numbly. I've never lived on my own before, so everything feels new. There are plenty of reasons to be freaked out about living on my own, so what's one more to add to the list?

By the second landing, we're laughing breathlessly at ourselves for attempting this feat.

"Can I help you with that?" Holt hefts the box into his capable arms before either of us can catch our breath long enough to answer.

Eden rolls her eyes, but the smile on her lips reminds me of what a good match the two of them are. Not only are they both drop-dead gorgeous, but they're also a highly intelligent pair, complementing each other in wit and work ethic. Basically, they're perfect together.

My chest tightens painfully behind my oversize T-shirt. I miss Alex. A lot. Even more than I thought I would.

It began on the car ride back to Boston, while listening to the radio. An old country love song came on, reminding me of him and his ridiculous singing on the way back from town that one day. Then that memory brought along even more memories of my birthday, of the lake, all our shared meals—not to mention the countless physical moments, from innocent cuddles to . . . well, all the rest of it.

The truth is, in the weeks since I left the cabin, I haven't been able to stop thinking about him and our summer of bliss, try as I may to distract myself with work and the move. I've even begun to question leaving the cabin while he was out on an errand, days before we were both due to leave. It was impulsive. And thinking back, maybe I should have just talked to him. Opened up and admitted everything.

When everything is upstairs, I spend a few minutes shuffling some new furniture around the apartment. Once I've moved a couple of end tables in the living room and shifted a small bookshelf to the bedroom, my place starts to look a lot classier. When I rejoin them, Holt and Eden are sharing a water bottle in the kitchen. My ears perk up when I realize they're talking about the team.

"They've all been checking in, one by one. Everyone's on their way back from wherever the hell they went this summer," Eden says with a wry smile. "You wouldn't believe where Saint went."

"The Cayman Islands?" Holt says, and we all laugh, knowing that could very well be true.

"The *Vatican.*" Eden emphasizes every syllable, and my eyes go wide with disbelief.

Holt chuckles, incredulous. "Yeah, I wouldn't have guessed that."

"I'm shocked he didn't burst into flames as soon as he set foot anywhere near a church," I say, earning a generous laugh from the couple.

I'm cracking open a water bottle for myself when Eden says, "Even Alex checked in."

My hands freeze on the plastic, all the blood in my body rushing into my reddening cheeks. I guzzle down the water until the bottle is totally empty, feeling a little light-headed. When I look back at Eden and Holt, they're both staring at me.

"Oh yeah?" I say, my voice cracking. I wipe some stray drops of water from my lips with the back of my hand.

A totally insane thought occurs to me. Did Alex tell Eden about our summer fling? He wouldn't, would he?

Eden nods. "Yeah, he texted me yesterday."

Do I jump through the window now, or what?

"What did he say?" I ask, trying my best at nonchalance.

She shrugs, using air quotes. "'Back in town.' I don't even get a full sentence from the man these days. Friggin' typical."

Relief trickles down my spine as excitement curls in my belly.

Back in town. Those three words thrum through

my veins. Odd to hear the news from Eden and not from the man himself, but it makes sense. I didn't exactly leave things on the best of terms, so it's not like he'd text me about his whereabouts.

Even if we're back to being strangers, I knew deep down that Alex wouldn't break my trust and tell Eden about our summer. Discretion was a major component of our arrangement. Alex is a good guy, despite Eden's grumblings. He wouldn't sabotage either of us like that.

"Anyway," Eden says, "can we help you unload some of . . ." She gestures vaguely around the apartment. "This?"

I don't have a lot of stuff, but unpacking will take an embarrassing amount of time. I'm kind of a perfectionist when it comes to my stuff, as little as there is, and everything has to have its proper place. I wouldn't subject my worst enemies, let alone my friends, to that level of micromanaging.

"No, you've helped me enough already. I don't think I have the energy to dive back into it right now, anyway. Can I order us a pizza or something?"

Holt and Eden exchange one of those *we're a couple so we can communicate with our eyes* looks before Holt says, "That won't be necessary. We have dinner reservations later. Thanks for the offer, though."

"And this is for you." Eden holds out a gift bag that clearly contains a bottle of wine. Knowing her, it's an expensive one. "Consider it a housewarming gift."

"Are you kidding? I consider *all* of this a house-warming gift."

"Well, this one you can drink." She shoots me a playful wink.

I accept the bag with a grateful sigh. "You guys are the best. Seriously, I don't know how I could have done it without both of you."

After we swap sweaty hugs and promises to see each other at work on Monday, I watch them make their way down the stairs. My eyes linger on Eden's hand, which rests comfortably between Holt's shoulder blades. For the first time in a while, I let myself feel joy for them and their happiness, not just jealousy of what they share, even if it is a constant reminder of how alone I really am.

My phone buzzes in my back pocket. It's my mom, checking in to see if now is a good time to chat.

Debating, I chew on my lip. I've kind of been avoiding her ever since the breakup. So, we haven't really talked all summer, at least not in a meaning-ful way. I was so afraid to tell her—a wife who could only be separated from her husband by the finality of death—that my only serious relationship failed so miserably. My shoulders sag, but I know now is as good a time as any.

I close the front door and latch it, navigating the war zone that is my apartment until I reach the window seat and settle in. My thumb hovers over CALL for a moment's hesitation. The phone rings a few times before she picks up.

"Hello, baby girl. Long time no chat."

I smile at the nickname, suddenly feeling like a little kid all over again. If only life were that sim-ple. "Hi, Mom. How are you?"

"Oh, you know. Busy as ever. That dang kids' camp had me running around like a crazy person, to no one's surprise. I finally got a membership at JoAnn's to help pay for all those craft supplies, and now they won't stop sending me emails."

She rambles on for a while longer, but I don't mind. Her voice is so comforting. I can't believe I waited so long to do this.

"Enough about me," she says with a dramatic sigh. "Tell me about you. How are you? How's Dale?"

His name still feels like a bullet through my heart, but the pain passes faster and faster each day.

I take a deep breath. "Actually, there have been some pretty big changes in my life that I need to fill you in on. Are you sitting down?"

It takes about thirty minutes, at least ten of which I spend crying, to explain everything to my mom. We cover the cheating, the breakup, the couch-surfing, the cabin . . . I even tell her about Alex.

Well, not *everything* about Alex. Certainly not about the sex. My mom has no business knowing about that time we fucked on the kitchen island. Or that other time I blew him on the deck. Now that I think about it, I'm not sure if there's a square inch on that property we didn't claim as our own sexual playground.

Don't think about it, Aspen.

"You'll have to come see me at the new place," I say, taking in all the cardboard boxes on the floor. "Once I'm more situated and settled in. It's a bit of a war zone at the moment."

"Well . . ." Her smile comes through, even over the phone. "Considering you never once invited me up to Boston when *you know who* was still in the picture, I must say that I'm pretty happy with these life changes. You sound more like yourself than you have in years. And I would love to come and visit and let you show me the city sights."

Tears prick at the corners of my eyes because I know she's right. Until recently, I was a version of myself that I didn't like. I was closed off to family and friends, preferring no contact to the reality of admitting how emotionally abusive my relationship was. I was always "too busy," choosing to drown myself in work rather than accept how unhappy my life had become.

"Yeah." I let out a trembling sigh. "I definitely feel more like myself these days, and it feels really good."

"That's all I've ever wanted. You know I love you, right? Even when you wait a while to tell me everything all at once. I love you no matter what."

"I love you too."

"Now, you let me know when there's someone special in the picture, all right?"

"Mom—"

"I know, I know. You don't *need* a man. It's just nice to have someone on your team, helping you get through life in one piece. God knows I miss your father every single day."

"I miss him too." I cradle my phone against my cheek, wiping a stray tear away with my thumb.

Will I ever have the kind of love that my parents shared? And if so, how long do I have to wait to meet him? Or have I met him already?

Beneath the insecurities and regrets, a name echoes in the recesses of my healing heart.

Alex Braun.

Mom and I say our good-byes with plans to make mother-daughter calls a biweekly thing. I hang up and silence wraps around me like a cashmere blanket.

I finally have a moment to myself to just sit and think, so I soak in my surroundings, as messy and stressful as they are. Out the window, the afternoon sun is starting to set, casting a golden glow across my floors. It's almost as if Boston is saying, *Welcome home, Aspen.*

This is my place. All mine. I don't have to inconvenience anyone else ever again. I don't have to share it with anyone.

Though I wouldn't mind sharing it from time to time with a certain hockey player by day, master chef by night, but I can't let myself imagine the possibilities. I've made my bed, and now I've got to lie in it.

As for what could have been? I guess I'll never know.

23

ALEX

After a grueling workout off the ice, the guys and I suited up in full gear and hit the ice for another hour of drills, and then listened to Coach Wilder give us an inspirational talk. At least, I think it was supposed to be an inspirational talk. But it's clear his drawn-out and very public divorce has messed with his head, because the dude was all over the place.

Our team captain, Reeves, jumped in and saved the day with an encouraging story that had us all laughing. And when you're dead tired and starving . . . laughter can be hard to come by. But Reeves is just that kind of guy. Everyone loves him.

Our first preseason game is in six days, and training camp is behind us. It's go-time, and for the most part, I'm feeling ready for the season to begin.

I told myself that this was my year. My time to shine. Time to leave all the bullshit from my past behind me. But I never counted on skating into this season with a broken heart.

I never meant to fall in love with Aspen.

But it is what it is, and I can't help how gutted I still feel. Finding her note and realizing she was gone . . . That was one of the hardest days of my life.

I've texted her a couple of times to say hello and see if she found a place to live. She's replied with one-word responses, or worse, the thumbs-up emoji. Like she couldn't even be bothered to type out a few basic words to appease me.

My somber thoughts are interrupted by Saint and Lucian, who have gotten into yet another argument about American politics. Annoyed, I decide I can't listen to them go back and forth for another second. Rising to my feet, I ball up a towel and throw it at Saint's head.

"Enough. You're both idiots. Neither one of you is American, and you can't vote, so drop it."

"Someone needs to get laid," Tate says, giving me a skeptical look.

I narrow my eyes at him.

Saint drops the towel into the laundry hamper and sits down on the bench next to me. "Everything . . . okay?"

I haven't spoken to him much since returning, other than to say a quick thank-you for offering his cabin for the summer. I've avoided him for good reason. He's a good enough friend that I'm sure he'll see right through me if I talk about my summer. The conversation is inevitable, but I'm just not ready to have it yet.

"*Fine.*" I growl out the word and finish lacing up my sneakers.

Saint doesn't look convinced. "You want to go get something to eat?"

"Sure," I say, since I am starving.

It's only after we're seated at the diner that Saint starts in with his questioning. "What happened this summer?"

I set the sticky menu down on the table and glare at him. "Nothing *happened.*"

"Come on, Braun. I know something must have happened. We've been friends for a couple years now, right?"

"I guess so."

He shrugs. "Which means I *know* you. And I know something happened."

Our waitress swings by the table, and we place our orders. Both of us get the same thing—double cheeseburgers minus the buns, and a side salad.

Saint flirts with the waitress, who lingers at our table longer than necessary. Then he swings his attention back to me. "Seriously, let's talk. Should I book an appointment at the tattoo parlor?"

"Fuck off," I grumble.

The truth is, I really can't answer Saint, because even I don't know what happened. I thought Aspen and I were building something, but then she left and ghosted me, and now we're back to practically being strangers. I hate that.

Saint unrolls his silverware from the napkin. "I'm not looking for the dirty details. I just want to know what's up with you. You hooked up with Aspen. You guys stayed up there together all summer, and now you're back and your mood is complete crap. I'm just . . . I'm here for you."

I release a slow exhale and finally look up to meet his concerned gaze. "Yeah. I hear you. The truth is, I guess I fell for her."

"Shit. Really?"

I nod. "Yeah. But all she wanted was a rebound fling. She's barely talking to me now."

"That sucks," he says, shaking his head. "I'm sorry, man."

I'm not even sure why I told him. Maybe I'm just tired of pretending this summer didn't happen. Tired of lying in bed at night with my phone, wishing a message would magically pop up from Aspen.

No longer hungry, I pick at my food. "I guess you won."

"I don't care about that."

I shrug. "A bet's a bet." Maybe the piercing pain of a tattoo gun would distract me from the all-encompassing pain in my chest.

Saint grins. "Then let's go get this tattoo, bro."

I smile for the first time today. "Yeah? You pick something out for me?"

"I've got just the thing."

When we leave the diner, we drive straight to a nearby tattoo parlor where I get an emoji face with heart eyes tattooed onto my left ass cheek.

The sore spot on my ass? It can only be summed up one way.

You play stupid games, you win stupid prizes.

24

ALEX

Waking up to over a thousand tweets, all featuring the hashtag #Banish-Braun, is an experience unlike any I've had before. I wouldn't wish it on my worst enemy.

With bleary eyes from a night of restless sleep, I read the tabloid headlines. Looks like the prosecution decided to play dirty. And as usual, the press took it and ran with it.

Braun Sued On Sexual Harassment Accusations

ALEX BRAUN — Bad Boy or Just A Bad Guy?

Braun's Harassment Victim Tells All: Her Night Out Turned Nightmare

A cold feeling sinks into my skin like an ice bath, freezing my insides. And yet my brain is boiling. *I didn't do this*, I want to scream. Instead, I sit alone in my house, sulking.

I want to call someone, to talk to a teammate or maybe family, but how do I talk about this?

Nelle wouldn't handle it well. I'm thankful she's not on social media these days, so maybe she hasn't heard yet. I can't trust Saint not to make some kind of joke, even well-intentioned, about the situation. And Aspen . . . well, Aspen and I aren't exactly on talking terms, are we?

My head throbs as I imagine her waking up to this news like I did, her hand flying up to her mouth to cover her gasp. I spiral into worst-case scenarios—Aspen believes the tabloids instead of me . . . Aspen regrets our time together . . . Aspen doesn't ever want to see me again. That last one stings the most.

I don't realize my hands are shaking until my phone buzzes in my grip. It's Eden. God, it's not even seven in the morning. Regret that I didn't tell her about the lawsuit before it exploded all over social media makes my head throb even more.

"Hey."

"Fucking hey. Get your ass to my office. Now!"

And just like that, Eden hangs up.

I toss my phone onto the bed and try to drown out the onslaught of notifications by shutting the bathroom door behind me and cranking the shower knob. After an icy shower, I somehow manage to make myself presentable, and I'm out the door. My heart is racing, but trying to slow my breathing only makes me dizzy. On the drive to the arena, I deal with the unpleasant task of calling my lawyer, Hugh.

• • •

When I arrive at the office, Eden's door is cracked open, but I knock anyway.

"Come in."

Without a greeting, I enter and seat myself across from Eden, who won't look at me. She just stares at her phone, scrolling through what I can only imagine is the wildfire of my already damaged reputation, burning to ash.

A minute crawls by in awkward silence. Finally, she meets my gaze. Her eyes are red-rimmed and furious.

"What the hell, Alex," she hisses, switching her dinging phone to silent.

I shake my head, feeling lower than I've ever felt before. "I'm sorry, Eden."

"Wanna tell me what the hell I've been reading all morning?" She raises her phone like a gavel.

"I should have told you—"

"Oh, so you knew this was happening? Great. Way to *blindside* me." Her voice isn't raised in any sense, but the words sting my ears as if she were yelling at the top of her lungs.

"I deserve that. I'm sorry."

Her scowl is pained. "For what?"

I take a deep, shaky breath. "I'm sorry for not telling you about the lawsuit as soon as I was told about the possibility of it happening."

Her scowl falls away, replaced with an anxious frown. "And are you sorry for anything else?"

There it is. The doubt. The uncertainty that I'm even half the man she thought I was.

"I didn't do it," I say firmly, but she's quiet. Her icy attitude toward me stings more than I expected it to. "And I need you to believe me, Eden. I wouldn't harass a woman. You know I'm not that guy."

She clears her throat. "I'm listening."

The truth comes out earnest and firm, but Eden's expression remains unchanged. What if this was the final deal breaker? What if this is the beginning of the end of my hockey career? Just the thought makes my stomach roll with nausea.

"I don't even care about my reputation right now. Kick me off the team, for all I care. If you need to do that, I would completely understand. But I just need you to know, I need you to believe that I would never—"

"Okay, Alex. Okay." Eden holds up a freshly manicured hand, silencing me. "Please stop."

When I do, the room fills with the faint sounds of my unsteady breathing. Another minute passes before she speaks again.

"I know you, okay? I've known you for almost seven years . . ." She blinks as if those words surprise her. "I know you would never do anything even remotely—"

The turmoil in my stomach stutters to a halt. "Thank y—"

"No, I'm not done. I do believe in you. But if you make me regret this decision, I will kill you with my bare hands. Do you understand?"

I know Eden as well as she knows me. The

woman isn't bluffing.

"I understand."

"Good. I've been wondering if the team should go through sexual harassment training again this season. This shit show settles it."

Now I'm confused. "Why? You just said you believe me."

"Alex." Eden sighs, closing her eyes as she pinches the bridge of her nose. "Whether you realize it or not, the team looks up to you. Especially the younger guys. I don't want this *one* instance of a woman lying getting the bigger issue twisted in their heads. This is not the norm. The vast majority of sexual harassment and assault reports are true."

I nod, a new understanding dawning on me. Now that the suit is a complete media circus, covered by tabloids, no less, people with the wrong idea could use my lawsuit as an example—hell, as *ammunition*—to shut down real victims in the future. I make a mental note to emphasize sensitivity toward the broader issue during my next call with Hugh.

Our conversation is far from over, but I feel like I can breathe easier now. Eden believes me. Maybe Aspen will too.

As if my very thought summoned her, Aspen walks through the door. It's been a month since I've seen her in person, a month since I felt that familiar swell in my heart at the sight of her.

Goddamn. In this case, reality is so much better than memories. She's beautiful.

"Hi, sorry I'm late. My car—" Aspen suddenly snaps her mouth shut, seeing me sitting across from Eden. "Oh . . . uh, hi, Alex."

"Hey." I can't help but stare at her.

The summer tan that once gave Aspen a smattering of freckles across her nose and cheeks has faded. It's strange seeing her in a button-up and pencil skirt instead of her usual oversize T-shirt and yoga pants. Her lips are painted that same muted rosy color she wore that night to the brewery—that night that felt a lot like a date. It's too painful to let myself think about, so I push it from my head.

"What's up with your car?" I hear myself ask.

"Oh." She scoffs, a nervous energy about her. "It wouldn't start."

"Do you need—"

"One of my neighbors helped me jump it."

Neighbor. Right. She has her own place now,

but I have no idea where. I have no idea if it's in a safe neighborhood, or if she has everything she needs. And with the way our brief time together ended, I may never know.

I nod once and turn my attention back to Eden. She's glowering at us like we've just made out in front of her. I wouldn't be surprised if she suspects something. And though I'm not ashamed of anything I did with Aspen, I'm a little concerned by the glare Eden is leveling at us right now.

"Have you seen the tabloids today, Aspen?"

Fuck.

Aspen sighs with a tired smile. "Oh God, what is it now?"

She doesn't know yet. I shoot Eden a pleading look. "Eden—"

"Our boy Alex here is being sued on sexual harassment allegations."

If I ever had a kind thought about this woman, it's long gone. *Dammit, Eden.*

I shake my head in disbelief. Eden just shrugs and turns back to her computer.

"What?" Paler than I've ever seen her, Aspen locks her wide eyes on me.

"It's not what you think—"

Eden clears her throat loudly, interrupting me. "Alex, would you mind giving us a moment? We have to, you know, clean up your mess."

I take a steadying breath before standing. I breeze past Aspen, desperate to put some space between us as quickly as possible. She was going to find out one way or another, but I wish it didn't happen like this.

25

ASPEN

efore entering the rink, I take a bracing breath, focusing on the stands instead of the burly bodies racing across the ice. I usually love watching the guys play, thriving in their element, but lately it's the last place that I want to be. It may have something to do with all the complicated feelings I have for their starting center.

Les, the front-office manager, waves to me from the sidelines, silver strands in his hair catching the light from the overhead lights. "Aspen. You have my files?"

"Yep. Eden says to reference the budget while you read, which is down at the bottom . . . here."

I open the application and pass the tablet off to Les, who mutters to himself while navigating the folder to view its contents. He struggles a little with technology, so I usually have to stay close in case he has questions. Sometimes I feel like I'm *his* assistant too. But I don't mind helping him, especially since Eden's ideal working pace is contingent on our tech literacy.

Once I feel like Les has a handle on what he's looking at, I lean against the rail to give him some space. Out of habit, my gaze wanders to the ice, and I immediately regret it.

A dozen other guys are on the ice warming up, but my gaze locks onto Alex instantly. He's running drills, his long and lean body equal parts grace and strength. I groan inwardly as I notice the familiar flutter in my chest. Gauging my heart rate and my inability to tear my gaze away, this is the opposite of what I need right now.

Passing the rookie, Alex flashes him an arrogant grin, and all the breath in my lungs seems to evaporate. The echo of his laugh carries across the ice and draws me deep into a memory.

Back at the cabin some months ago, Alex and I were lying naked on the floor in front of the fire, with nothing but a shared fleece blanket between us. I remember him playing with a strand of my hair, tickling my shoulder with it.

"Stop it." I giggled, burying my face against his chest.

"Should I?" Even though I couldn't see his expression, I could hear the smirk in his voice. That cocky growl reserved for quiet, skin-to-skin moments.

"Yes," I said with a chuckle. "But keep holding me, okay?"

"Always," he whispered, wrapping his solid arms tighter around me, our bodies so warm and comfortable that I forgot for a moment that we were once two separate people.

Now, with yards of cold air between us, it's never been clearer how separate we really are.

"I'm all done," Les says, appearing at my side. "Thanks for your help. These contraptions are going to be the death of me, I swear."

I smile, taking the tablet. "I'll upload it all to the cloud so you can have access to it whenever you want, okay?"

"I've never thought of clouds as particularly accessible, but . . ." He grins at me with a twinkle in his eye, and I chuckle, giving him a nod before I turn back toward the exit.

"Hey. Aspen, hold up!" Alex's voice cuts

through the scrape of skates against the ice.

I think about pretending not to hear him and hurrying toward the door to make a swift escape. But I don't want the team to notice that anything's off. So instead, I stop in the shadowy alcove and wait until Alex joins me. His cheeks are flushed with exertion, his blue eyes bright. He brushes sweat-soaked hair from his forehead.

"Hey," I manage to say, hugging the tablet close to my chest.

"Thanks for stopping by. It's good to see you."

"Yeah, of course. Do you need something?"

"Ah, no, actually," he grunts outs. "I was wondering if *you* need anything. You know, for the new place? Is there anything I could help you with?"

A rogue smile pulls at the corner of my mouth, but I quickly hide it by tucking a strand of hair behind my ear. "I've got a good setup. Thanks, though."

"Of course. You know you can call me if you need anything, right? Like when your car broke down, I would have been happy to . . . Aspen, can you look at me?"

I reluctantly meet his gaze, despite the fact that I know I'm a goner under those blue eyes. As expected, they do their work on me, shining slivers of light through the cracks in the invisible wall between us.

"Sorry," I say, my voice colder than I mean it to be. "But I've got it covered."

"Are you . . . upset with me?" he asks, his brow furrowed.

"No, I'm not upset with you." I didn't realize the words were true until I said them. If I'm not upset, then what exactly *am* I feeling?

Love, a voice in my head whispers knowingly.

Love, even though you know he doesn't feel the same way.

Love, even though he didn't think to share something as big as the lawsuit with you, even when you were sharing the same bed.

Love, even though it hurts you.

Why can't love ever be simple in my life? Why does it always come with complications and caveats? Why all the pain?

I squeeze my eyes closed, searching for the right way to phrase this. "It's more that I'm confused, Alex. Why didn't you tell me about the lawsuit? I mean, it began back when we were—" I cut myself off, choosing my next words carefully. "When we were in Canada. I just don't understand why you kept it a secret from me."

It takes him a moment to respond. While I wait, I let myself admire the features I've spent weeks trying to forget. That mess of brown hair. Those heavy eyebrows guarding vulnerable eyes. The sharp line of his jaw and the soft curve of his lips, which finally open to speak.

"Yeah." Alex sighs, running a hand down his face. "About that. I'm sorry for not telling you. I don't know what I was thinking. I guess I was just trying not to ruin our time together."

"How would the truth have ruined our time together?"

A muscle twitches in his jaw, and he shakes his head in frustration. "I don't know if you've noticed, Aspen, but in general, people don't really like me. Or even know me at all. But you took the chance to get to know me, and I—I guess I didn't want you to think of me any differently."

"But you see why that's confusing to me, right? You didn't give me the same chance that I gave you. You didn't give me the chance to be there for you. All I'm saying is that you should have told *me* before you told Eden."

Holy hell, I just sounded crazy jealous.

Alex's eyes flash at his ex's name, trained on mine before they soften, drifting to my lips. I've seen that face. This man desperately wants to kiss me.

"You're right."

"You say that I know you, but I'm not sure anymore."

"You do, Aspen. You do know me. Maybe better than anyone else."

Alex is so close to me now, our shadows bleed together into the darkness of the corner we're hiding in. His expression is open and vulnerable.

How many other people have seen this side of him? His teammates, definitely not. Eden? Probably just glimpses. Maybe I do know him best. God, we're so close. If we were to kiss, no one would know. It would be our little secret . . .

Just like our summer arrangement. And look where that got us.

I don't want to be his dirty little secret. I can't do that anymore.

I try to take a step back from him, but my feet won't budge. So, I retreat with my words.

"You should have told me about the lawsuit. Not just as your friend, but as your colleague." I trip up on the word *friend*, the bluntness of it feeling like a lie.

You don't sleep with friends. I don't, at least. Not anymore.

"I know. I'm sorry. I fucked up," he says sincerely, and I believe him.

"Thanks for apologizing," I murmur, my hand twitching at my side. I want to reach out and touch him. I want that intimacy we had back in Canada.

"Thanks for letting me. Hell, thanks for believing me."

As if he had the very same thought, Alex reaches for my hand and laces our fingers together. His palm is rough and warm, instantly thawing my chilled skin. I melt into a puddle at the overwhelming sense of belonging that I feel at his touch.

This can't happen, Aspen.

With the pending lawsuit and Eden's repeated warnings, all signs point toward disaster. I can't risk the fallout. If I learned anything from dating Dale, it was to trust a red flag when I see it.

"Yeah, well, Eden believes you, so why shouldn't I?"

A complicated expression comes over his face when, speak of the devil, my phone rings.

I wrench my hand free from his and pull my phone out of my back pocket, lifting it to my ear. "Hey, Eden."

"Hey. Sorry to make you run around like a crazy person, but I just thought of another errand you could knock out for me. Can you head back up to the office when you're done with Les?"

"Sure, I'll be right there," I say, then tuck the phone back in my pocket.

Alex gives me a solemn look.

"I'd better go," I tell him.

With one last look of longing, I turn on my heel and head for the staff elevator.

I think that short exchange was meant to be *the conversation* where we clear the air between us for good. But I've never felt foggy. And though I have a sneaking suspicion that Alex is still standing there, watching me walk away, I keep my eyes locked on what's ahead of me.

Keep moving, Aspen. Just keep moving forward.

26

ALEX

We've won our first six games of the season, and tonight, the entire team is ready to celebrate. Saint is hosting a party at his place—just a low-key get-together for the team and their significant others.

I finish getting ready and grab the bottle of expensive champagne I've had chilling in the fridge. Because I have another thing to celebrate tonight too. The sexual harassment lawsuit I was stressing over finally got dropped today. My name has been almost completely vindicated in the press too, now that the truth is out. *Hallelujah*. I also found a new agent after firing Kyle the douche.

"Thanks for coming," Saint says, greeting me at the front door when I arrive twenty minutes later.

"Thanks for hosting." I hand him the bottle of

champagne, and he nods.

"Come on in. Food and drinks are in the kitchen. Help yourself. PlayStation tournament in the basement, and cigars out on the deck."

"Okay, cool. Thanks, man."

Saint's been there for me these past few weeks, ever since I admitted to him the depth of my feelings for Aspen . . . and got that awful tattoo.

I definitely want to check out this PlayStation tournament, but first I need something to drink, so I head to the kitchen. Tate and Reeves are seated at the island, munching on appetizers.

"Hey," I say, tipping my chin in their direction before scoping out the beer situation.

The yellow label on one bottle sends a jolt down my spine. It's the same brand Aspen and I enjoyed last summer at that brewery in Ottawa. I grab a Budweiser instead and twist off the top.

"Dude, you've got to try one of these," Tate says to me, holding out a paper plate.

"What is it?" I take a step closer.

"Heaven in your mouth. That's what it is."

I grab one of the appetizers from the plate—it appears to be bacon and puff pastry. And when I chew, I catch a hint of fig too. It would have paired wonderfully with that grapefruit IPA. Instead, I choke down another swig of Bud.

"Thanks," I mutter.

Tate and Reeves carry the conversation, and aside from some well-timed grunts and the occasional nod, I'm barely hanging on.

I didn't expect to see Aspen tonight. But she arrived a few minutes ago, tagging along with Eden and Holt. Ducking her chin to avoid meeting my eyes, she shuffled past the kitchen where I've planted myself near the food—because the rookie was right, these bacon-fig things are amazing.

But one look at Aspen, and I've forgotten how to breathe, much less chew.

At least she showed up single. I wouldn't have handled it very well if she'd walked in on some other guy's arm.

Even though I'm trying to participate in whatever topic it is that Tate and Reeves have moved on to, I'm distracted. I can overhear Aspen telling a story to Eden, and I'm dying to know what has her so animated. I steal a look every few seconds over to where she's standing by the couch.

"I wanted to reevaluate every life choice I'd

ever made," Aspen says with a wave of her hand. "Seriously. It was one of those moments where I wanted to just leave quietly, hanging my head."

Eden chuckles, and shame burns hotly through me.

Could she be talking about our summer together?

God, I hope not. But what if she is? What if she doesn't have any of the fond memories I do about our time in Canada?

The idea of that cuts deep. But the only way to know is to talk to her. First, I'm going to need something stronger to drink.

Fortified by a few sips of expensive whiskey, I've talked myself into going to say hello. But since Aspen's no longer in the living room, I go off in search of her.

First, I check downstairs. A few of the guys are lounging on sectional sofas, playing video games on Saint's giant flatscreen. And Eden is down here too, talking to Lucian and his wife, Camille. But no Aspen.

Next, I decide to check outside on the back deck. It takes my eyes a moment to adjust to the darkness. Even with the soft landscape lighting and nearly full moon, it's pretty dark out here.

Holt and Saint are sitting in cushy club chairs, finishing cigars. And Aspen is leaning against the railing of the deck.

My heart gives a painful lurch.

She looks beautiful. Her long hair is loose and wavy, and while she's dressed casually in a pair of jeans and a fleece sweater, she still takes my breath away.

"Aspen," I say, nodding once in her direction.

"Hi, Alex," she says, her tone even and reserved.

"What's up, buddy?" Saint asks. "You come out to have a cigar?"

"No." I shake my head. "Just wanted some air."

He nods. Aspen looks contemplatively out at the backyard, not acknowledging my presence.

It's quiet for a minute, and the air around us is seasoned by the pungent aroma of tobacco.

"Hey, have I ever shown you the painting I bought at auction?" Saint says, looking at Holt.

Holt gives him a confused look. "No?"

Saint stands and gestures for him to follow. "Oh, it's sweet. Come see."

They head inside, leaving Aspen and me alone.

"So," I say awkwardly, turning to face her.

Aspen gives me a weak smile. "So."

It's the first time we've been alone together in so long. My hands itch to reach out and touch her, to hug her warm body to mine so I can press my lips to her hair.

"How have you been?" I say instead.

"Fine. You?"

I nod. "Good."

"That's good."

Fuck, this is so awkward.

"The season's been going well," Aspen says.

"Have you been watching the games?" I'm not sure why, but the idea that maybe she's been watching me play is a nice thought.

"Some of them," she says, quickly meeting my eyes before looking away again.

I inhale and straighten my shoulders. "Listen, I never wanted things to be strained between us. Can we just . . ."

"Just what?" she asks.

"Be friends." The words are literally painful leaving my mouth. It's the last thing I want.

"Of course," she says.

She doesn't look nearly as affected as I feel. Her posture is relaxed, and her tone is even. Meanwhile, I feel like I'm drowning, unable to get enough oxygen into my lungs.

"So, you came to the party alone?" I ask. It's a leading question, and Aspen knows this.

"So did you," she says. "Although, I figured you would have moved on by now."

Her words slice through me. That may have been my reputation before, jumping from one woman to the next, but it's not who I am anymore.

"Well," I say slowly, "some things you just don't get over."

When Aspen's eyes lift to mine, understanding flashes through them.

"And another thing . . . the reason I didn't tell you about the lawsuit," I say, my voice tight. "I was afraid of letting you down."

"Alex, you wouldn't have—"

Not letting her finish that sentence, I take a step closer and lift her chin before fusing my mouth to hers. Emotion flares inside me, but I can do nothing but stand here, tasting her mouth as her fists curl into the front of my shirt.

"I missed you. I missed us," I murmur between kisses.

"I can't," she chokes out.

And then she's gone—turning and heading inside before I can even process what just happened.

• • •

Standing at my ex's front door the next morning, I glare at her. "What the hell did you tell Aspen about me?"

Eden's expression is wary. "Good morning to you too."

Seeing how quickly Aspen shut me down last night when I admitted I missed her had me thinking there must be more to the story. Which is why I've driven over to my ex's house this morning in search of answers. And I'm not leaving here until I get them.

"I'm serious, Eden. I need to know."

She swallows hard. "You'd better come in and sit down."

"Coffee?" Holt asks, appearing from the kitchen.

"Sure," I say.

Once he's poured three mugs of coffee, he joins us in the living room. They settle onto the sofa together while I take a chair across from them.

"Well?" I ask impatiently.

Eden takes in a deep breath and then lets it out slowly. "You know Aspen worked with me back when you and I were ending things. And I may not have always painted an accurate picture of you. I was hurt, and I didn't hide my feelings from my assistant."

Resisting the urge to roll my eyes, I take a sip of coffee instead.

Giving me a curious look, Eden asks, "Did she say something, or . . ."

I rake a hand through my hair and sigh. "Not really. She's barely speaking to me right now. And she seems to have a bunch of shit in her head about why we'd never work."

"You like her," Eden says softly.

I don't hesitate. "Very much."

Holt watches us silently as Eden's mouth twitches with a smile.

"It's probably my fault," she says. "I'll talk to her. Okay?"

I shrug. This whole conversation is just weird. Talking to my ex in front of her fiancé, and telling her I like her assistant. It's like a soap opera.

"Would that help?" Eden leans forward, meeting my eyes. And I can tell, she really does want to help. It's something, at least.

"I don't know," I admit. "It couldn't hurt."

Holt takes her hand and gives it a gentle squeeze as a look of understanding passes between them.

There's a lot of history between Eden and me, but none of the loving fondness that these two share. It's obvious they're perfect for each other, and the more I'm around them, the more I believe it. I could never have given Eden everything she wanted, just like I know she couldn't give me everything I needed.

"How did you know that Holt was your forever?"

Eden smiles, crossing one leg over the other. "We were eating popcorn at the movies. He looked at me and smiled, and I knew I didn't want to eat popcorn with anyone else ever again."

"Damn."

She laughs, her eyes twinkling. "Yeah. I know."

Holt squeezes her hand, and they share a sweet look.

I take another sip of coffee. Maybe it's long overdue for us to be having this conversation. Or maybe we just weren't ready until now. I'm not sure, but I know it has to happen for the sake of our working relationship, as well as any possible friendship we might have in the future.

"I know why you and I never worked. You needed a project. Someone to save. And I didn't need saving, Eden."

She offers me a sad smile. "No, I guess you didn't."

"I just needed someone to be there to cheer me on."

I also needed someone who didn't need anything from me. Who could just . . . *be.* And that girl wasn't Eden. She was constantly striving for more, always daydreaming of her next big idea, the next project. I guess she gets that with Holt. The guy seems like he could use someone in his corner.

It's another reason why I know that Aspen is perfect for me. She doesn't have the constant need for speed that Eden does. Chill in Canada all summer on a whim? She was down. Jump into a freezing-cold lake? Why not?

God, I miss Aspen. I miss talking to her. Cooking for her. Holding her. Making love to her. I miss the person I was when I was with her.

"I'm going to talk to her, okay?" Eden says, interrupting my thoughts.

"Okay," I say with a nod.

"Maybe it'll help."

"Maybe."

Even if it is a big maybe, I have some hope for the first time in a long time. And hope is a very good thing. I have no idea how, but I'm going to show Aspen how good we could be together.

But first, I'm going to call Saint, because a man needs a plan.

27

ASPEN

When I first learned that our annual charity gala would be held in a historic hotel downtown, I was excited to attend because it would give me the chance to get dressed up and sip champagne. But once I realized the chances of seeing Alex here were statistically high, I wasn't sure I should come.

Now that I'm here, though, I'm determined to make the best of it.

The cold fall air retreats as soon as I step inside the ballroom, which is filled with beautifully dressed people in evening gowns and tuxedos. I'm wearing a rose-colored number that I rented from a bridal shop down the street from my apartment. The long sleeves are made of sheer lace, the bodice accentuating my breasts with a delicate pearl outline. The lengthy skirts trail behind me slightly, so I hike them up with one hand, revealing the four-inch nude heels that I'm already regretting.

"This is incredible," I murmur, reaching out to touch Eden's arm.

She turns to me and smiles, absolutely stunning in her *Vogue*-worthy black velvet gown and matching gloves. "Honestly? Not as impressive as last year." She sighs, plucking a flute of champagne from a passing caterer's tray and bringing it to her red lips for a generous swig.

"I see Les," Holt says from behind us, towering over our heads. He's wearing a black tuxedo with velvet lapels, matching Eden.

I follow his gaze to a small gathering of familiar faces. That's when I see *him*, and my heart gives a painful little leap.

Even though he's got his back turned to us, I immediately recognize the familiar line of Alex Braun's broad back through his fitted suit jacket. It hugs his shoulders possessively, and though I can barely catch glimpses of him through the moving crowd, I know he looks absolutely dashing.

My stomach turns itself into an intricate knot. I can't face him tonight. My feelings for him are too big, too overwhelming.

I don't know how long I've been standing dumbstruck in the entrance until I realize Eden and Holt have abandoned me to join the gathering.

"Aspen!" a man's voice calls out from behind me.

I turn to see Reeves, one of the defensemen and the captain of the Titans, dressed in a navy-blue suit, the top few buttons of his white shirt purposely unbuttoned. He clearly saw the dress code as a loose guideline and ran with it.

"Fashionably late, I see," I tease.

"Always. So, what do you think of your first gala?" He looks around, his blue eyes twinkling.

"I feel out of place," I say with a sheepish grin.

He scoffs, stepping back to give me a thorough once-over with an appraising look. "You fit right in." He nods approvingly with a humorous glint in his eye.

I laugh, releasing some of the tension in my chest. "Thank you. Most of the crew is over there . . ."

I trail off, spotting another familiar face over Reeves' shoulder. Logan Tate, the rookie defenseman, is on the phone as he paces along the perimeter of the ballroom, frowning at the floor.

Reeves turns to follow my gaze. "Ah, shit," he says with a sigh, shaking his head mournfully.

"What's wrong?" I ask. I'm pretty clueless when it comes to drama on the team.

"His girlfriend—you know, the one from his hometown? I heard they just broke up. That's probably her, begging him to take her back."

"Oh no." I frown, squinting across large room to see if I can read his expression, but it's no use. I silently wish him luck handling whatever mess he's found himself in.

Welcome to the heartbreak club, rookie.

"This is exactly why I say relationships are overrated."

I roll my eyes at Reeves. "How would you know? You've never been in one."

He chuckles. "Weird. You sound just like my mother."

I spot Alex again, moving closer this time, and my head spins. I'm not ready to see him. Before I can think of a better course of action, I make a break for it.

"I have to find the restroom," I call over my shoulder. From the look on Reeves' face, he knows that I'm avoiding someone or something.

I weave through the crowd of rich socialites, doing my best not to step on anyone's skirt or Louboutin. When I see a sign marked RESTROOMS, I make a beeline for it.

Once inside, I finally let out a slow breath as my gaze sweeps over the wood paneling on the walls and complimentary toiletries on the countertop. A restroom attendant nods politely as I pass by her.

I stumble into a stall and latch the door behind me, taking deep, sobering breaths. I haven't had a sip of alcohol tonight, but it feels like my head is swimming. My phone buzzes in my clutch and I pull it out, my throat constricting at the sight of Alex's name.

You okay?

I feel like I could cry. I love this man so much, it's killing me. Why did I think getting close to him was a good idea? I'm such a fool.

A light knock rattles my stall door.

"Aspen?"

I blink, recognizing the voice as Eden's, and crack open the door. "Hey, what's up?"

"Can we talk?" she asks, her voice uncharacteristically soft.

I nod once. I'm sure my feelings for Alex are written all over my face. Eden's so intuitive, she must know.

Dutifully, I follow her out of the restroom and to the exit. We step outside into the crisp autumn air, and turn around to watch the party from a distance.

"What's going on?" I ask her, my deepest fears mounting with every passing second.

Did Alex tell her about us? Did she find out some other way? Am I about to be fired?

God, I hope not. I just signed a new lease.

She takes a deep breath before she begins. "I owe you an apology. I know that I can talk a lot of shit. I know that I blur the lines between our friendship and working relationship every day. I also know that isn't fair to you, although I think I only really understood that recently."

I stare at her, my mouth twisting into a frown. *What is she talking about?*

She meets my confused expression with a defeated sigh. "All I'm saying is that I may have been wrong about Alex."

Oh.

"I'm sorry if I led you to believe that he was disloyal or unfaithful. It was nothing like that. Alex never cheated on me or gave me any reason to think that he would. We were just two people who weren't built for the long haul. We broke up because we wanted different things. I spent years of my life supporting him, following him wherever the game took him, cheering for him from the sidelines. Over time, I fell out of love with him, but not because of anything he did wrong. I just eventually realized that I was loving him in the way I wanted to be loved. I wanted someone in my corner to support me and my life goals and career. By falling out of love with Alex, I fell in love with hockey, and I found my forever love with Holt."

I listen to Eden's confession, hanging on every word. I can tell by the misty look in her eyes that none of this is easy for her to admit.

"Meanwhile, Alex had already accomplished most of his goals, so he was looking for someone to settle down with. He couldn't keep up, and I couldn't slow down. I resented him for it. I felt like he owed me a fraction of what I gave him. I still feel that, to this day, but now I have Holt."

Eden's eyes shine with unshed tears, and a contagious smile breaks out across her face. I don't realize I'm crying too until a fat tear rolls down my cheek.

"And if I hadn't ended things with Alex, I would have never given Holt a chance. It's the best decision I ever made." She sighs contentedly, spinning the engagement ring on her finger. Shaking herself out of her reverie, she laughs breathlessly and nudges me with her shoulder. "All that to say Alex wasn't right for me. But that doesn't mean he's wrong for you."

She does know. Maybe she has all along, since that first video conference I had with her in Canada when she spotted him in the background of the screen.

I take a shuddering breath, releasing it with a heavy sigh of relief. With only a few words, Eden has lifted the weight I've been carrying around for weeks.

"Why did you decide to tell me all of this?" I ask, searching her expression for answers.

She giggles a little, almost embarrassed. "Alex actually came to see us. To talk about you. And he called me out for all the ideas I put in your head about him."

"He did?" My voice catches in my throat.

"Yeah. And based on the way that he's looking at you tonight, he's a man who's hurting." She nods toward the building, which is all lit up and filled with happy partygoers.

My heart squeezes with nerves. "Do you think I should go talk to him?"

"Only if you want to." Eden leans over and kisses me on the cheek.

Do I want to talk to him?

The realization crumbles inside me like a warm cookie straight from the oven. *Of course I do.* I've never wanted anything more in my life.

"Okay, let's go." I link my arm through hers, and we make our way back inside.

28

ALEX

I tug at the collar on my shirt again. I hate wearing a tuxedo, even if it's for a good cause. Tonight's the charity gala for the Children's Haven project the team supports. It's an event I've looked forward to in the past—the chance to stuff myself from the buffet and drink free booze . . . the chance to hang out with the team away from the ice.

But tonight, I'm all kinds of on edge.

Having Saint with me helps, I guess. He decided not to bring a date, and offered to give me a ride.

"You okay, buddy?" he asks from beside me.

I straighten my tie and nod distractedly. "Sure."

The ballroom is buzzing with excitement, and there's a long line at the bar, which I eye with disdain.

Saint brings one arm around my shoulders and leans in. "Okay, so let's talk game-plan strategy. Here's what we're going to do."

"We?" I stiffen.

Saint chuckles, and the sound vibrates between us. "Yes. *We*. I'm helping you."

I step back to meet his eyes with a look of confusion. After all, he's the one who warned me not to fall for her. "But why?"

He gives me a kind look. "Because you love her."

I make an exasperated noise. His words are true, and I'm tired of denying it. "Okay, fine. What's the plan?"

His mouth breaks into a happy grin. "First, we have to locate her. Are you sure she's going to be here?"

"She'll be here." I'm not sure why I'm so confident, because she could have changed her mind about coming tonight. Somehow, though, I can sense that she's here. Somewhere in the crowd of people.

Saint nods. "Okay, while we locate her, do you

want to get a drink? Some liquid courage?"

"No, I'm good." I'd rather have a clear head. And I don't want to waste time standing in line at the bar.

Saint nods. "Okay. We're going to figure this out. Let's head in."

The crowd parts as we make our way into the ballroom. A glittering chandelier hangs overhead, painting everything in gold hues. The setting would be romantic in any other circumstance. But I'm not optimistic enough for all that right now.

When we move past the banquet tables displaying items up for auction, something makes me turn. And then I see her.

Aspen.

She's wearing a pale pink gown with lace sleeves. It's so Aspen. Feminine, simple, and fun. My chest aches at the sight of her.

I elbow Saint's side. "There she is. I'll see you later."

His hand grips my shoulder, and he pulls me back a step. "Hey. Hold up. What's your plan?"

"I'm going to talk to her."

He frowns. "That won't work. What else you

got?"

"Ask her to get a drink?"

"Negative, cowboy. No one wants to wait in that line. Go ask her to dance. She's practically standing on the dance floor, and she's polite, so she won't be able to say no."

That might actually work. "Good plan."

He grins. "I know. Go get her, tiger."

It's only when I approach Aspen that I realize she's standing with Holt and Eden at the edge of the dance floor.

"Good evening," I say, tipping my chin at them.

"Hey, Alex," Eden says, smiling at me, and Holt shakes my hand.

Aspen looks nervous, but so fucking gorgeous that I almost forget how to breathe.

"Aspen, you look absolutely breathtaking."

She dips her chin, then lifts her eyes to mine. "Thank you."

"Care to dance?"

"Um . . ." She hesitates for half a second before Eden gives her a little shove toward me.

"You should. People never dance at these things."

"Okay," Aspen says, meeting my eyes again.

I offer her my hand and lead her to the center of the dance floor. The band is playing some slow-tempo thing that's perfect, because with all the confusing thoughts and emotions swirling through my head, I doubt I'll be able to do a little more than shuffle my feet.

The familiarity of her in my arms is disorienting. I've dreamed about her and imagined this a hundred times. But now that she's standing here, her palm on my bicep, my hand at her waist, her lovely scent intoxicating me . . . I'm careful to keep a respectful distance between us before I completely lose my head.

"I'm just going to say something here," I say, my voice a little uncertain. "I had an amazing time with you this summer. And this past month has been really hard."

Aspen's gaze lifts to mine. "I guess I shouldn't have just left like that. I had an amazing time too. I probably owed you a good-bye."

Nerves suddenly kick in, and I swallow. "Yeah, maybe, but here's the thing. I've been trying to respect the idea that you wanted a rebound fling, but

I don't want to let you just walk away."

She stiffens in my arms. "Are you saying you didn't want things to end?"

"I should have told you how I felt about you this summer. I messed everything up, letting you just walk away. Will you let me fix this?"

"How?"

I take a deep breath. "I don't know. But I want to be with you. Will you let me try?"

She meets my eyes with a cautious expression. "It's not going to be like it was this summer, you know? We were isolated from everything and everyone. We got to just exist in this perfect bubble where reality didn't seem to exist. Real life is hard."

I nod and touch her cheek with my thumb. "I know. I know it's not going to be easy all the time. I know that I travel a lot during the season, and that's not really fair to you. But I want you in my life. I need you in my life."

Her eyes glisten with unshed tears, but she doesn't say anything.

"Will you say something? Tell me what you're thinking."

Aspen lifts on her toes and presses her sweet

mouth to mine. The kiss almost knocks me off my feet. It was the last thing I expected.

"Yes," she murmurs when she pulls back. She wipes her lipstick from my upper lip.

I laugh and pull her into my arms. "Yes?"

"Yes, I'll be with you."

"Thank fucking God." Emotion rocks through me. It's the best fucking news in the world.

When her lips touch mine again, I abandon the idea of dancing altogether. Before I realize what's happening, I'm leading her someplace far, far away from all the people and the crowds. Someplace private where I can kiss her properly like I've ached to do for so many weeks.

With my hands full of Aspen, I duck around a corner, pleased when I see a sign for a door that reads HOSPITALITY SUITE. I'm just about to let us inside when a hand on my shoulder stops me.

It's Tate, the rookie, and he's wearing a knowing smile. "Where are you two sneaking off to?"

"Just cover for us, okay?" I give him a pointed look.

Tate's mouth lifts in a grin, and he rubs one hand over the stubble on his jaw. I've always liked

the guy, but if he gives me a hard time about this
. . .

"Wait." Aspen's eyes widen.

This hallway is deserted, but the sound of the band and low voices from beyond remind us that we are far from alone. But when I run my hand from her upper arm and into her hair, turning her face to mine for another kiss, her protests turn to soft whimpers.

"Just for a minute. I need to kiss you."

She nods, her hazy eyes locked on mine.

"Tate, guard the door," I bite out, and then lead Aspen inside.

The room is dark, but I find the light switch. It's set up like a hotel suite, with a small kitchenette and dining table that we bypass on our way to the sofa. But we only make it halfway there, because I press her up against the back of the couch and take her mouth again.

She tastes like champagne. My heart is so full of happiness, I might burst.

"Baby, I'm sorry for everything. I hated losing you. I hated how I treated you this summer," I murmur, my lips on her throat. "After that first night, when I told you it was a mistake . . . I was wrong."

"I'm sorry I left," she breathes out.

Aspen's hands are all over me, and when she palms the front of my dress pants, I bite out a groan.

I cup her face in my hands and bring her eyes to mine. "Should we go slow? I don't want to rush you."

Her mouth twitches with a smile. "There's no such thing as slow with you."

She's right. Everything is zero to a hundred with us. I'm convinced this woman was made just for me. And when she falls to her knees at my feet and begins working open the front of my pants, I know she is.

The first wet stroke of her tongue against me makes my chest hitch. I love that she loses all control around me, just like I do with her. I touch her hair and tell her how good this feels.

From her jeweled clutch on the floor, I hear a sound. With pleasure shooting through my veins, it takes me a second to realize Aspen's phone is ringing.

At first, she ignores it, continuing to suck and lick and nibble at my rigid flesh. I clench my hands into fists at my sides and let out a groan. But then Aspen pulls back and rummages through her purse until she can bring the phone to her ear.

"Hello?" She's breathless and her cheeks are flushed.

I gaze down at her, my dick hanging out of my pants, wanting to strangle whoever it is that interrupted us.

"It's Eden," she whispers, looking up at me from the floor. "Yes, um, uh-huh," she says, running her finger along my length teasingly.

I can't resist touching her cheek and guiding myself back into her mouth. She sucks on me, one long deep suck that makes my toes curl, before pulling back.

She gives me a stern look and whispers, "You're going to get me fired."

I take the phone from her hand and press the speakerphone button, because if there was ever a time to use the hands-free feature, it's now.

Aspen licks my cock, and all the breath leaves my lungs at once.

Eden is saying something, but all my focus is on Aspen and her hot mouth.

"I was just worried about you," Eden says. "You disappeared. Did Alex talk to you?"

Aspen releases me with a faint sound, her hand still stroking. "Um, yes, we're together right now."

"Oh," Eden says, sounding a little stilted. "I'm interrupting, aren't I?"

"In a manner of speaking," Aspen says.

"Okay, gross. Hanging up now."

I press a button to end the call and toss the phone onto the couch as Aspen looks up at me, a laugh on her lips.

"Did that just happen?"

I chuckle too. "Uh, yeah."

We're still laughing when Tate knocks on the door. "You guys okay in there?"

I sigh, realizing it's time to admit defeat. I help Aspen to her feet and unceremoniously tuck myself back into my pants. "We should probably go. Can we ditch the gala? Will you come home with me?"

She nods, smiling. "Lead the way."

• • •

Aspen's never been to my place, and so I really

can't fault her for wanting the full tour. Even if my body is unhappy about being abandoned in the middle of a blow job. I show her around, hurrying her through the home gym, kitchen, living room . . .

"You have a pool?" she asks excitedly, leaning close to the windows so she can see outside in the darkness.

"Yup. I've only been in it once, though."

"We are totally having a pool party here this summer."

"Yeah? You want to stay here, instead of Canada?"

She turns to look at me. "That was pretty perfect, wasn't it?"

"It was special. But I think we can make our own special traditions here too."

It's then that I know I want Aspen to move in with me. But since I'm smart enough not to get into what could turn into a lengthy discussion, I take her hand and tug her toward the stairs. We'll talk about that later.

"Last stop on the tour," I joke when we enter my bedroom.

"This is amazing," she says, scanning the room.

"Can you stay all weekend?" I pull her into my arms and wrap her in a hug. "I don't have a game until Tuesday night."

"I might be able to do that," she says playfully.

"We have some lost time to make up for."

Between soft, sweet kisses, I help Aspen out of her dress. She tugs at my jacket, and I remove it. And as she undoes each of the buttons on my shirt, I walk us backward toward the bed.

Once she's naked and in my arms, I have to remind myself to slow down, that we have all night . . . and that I want this to be perfect for her.

But then I hear a soft chuckle, and I meet Aspen's gaze.

She touches my tattoo. "Is this new?"

I guess it's time to come clean. "Uh, so I might have lost a bet."

Aspen laughs. "Oh?"

"Yeah. Saint bet me that I couldn't go the summer without falling in love with you."

She raises one eyebrow.

"And when I got home . . . I told him we'd better go get that tattoo."

She touches my cheek, her eyes filled with emotion.

"Aspen, what I'm saying is that I fell in love with you in Canada. I love you."

"I love you too," she says softly.

It feels good to say the words, to finally admit to Aspen how I really feel. And it feels even better to *show* her, and that's exactly what I spend the next hour doing. Long, and hard, and deeply until she's flushed and panting out my name.

Then I fold her into my arms and hold her close. All night long.

EPILOGUE

ASPEN

"**C**an I help?"

I sidle up to the kitchen island, leaning over the polished wood to showcase my cleavage in the long-sleeved romper I'm wearing. Alex looks up from where he's chopping vegetables, his gaze pinging between my face and my breasts.

"Eyes up here, Braun." I wink, walking my fingers toward him, and he playfully swats them away.

"No stray fingers near the sharp knife," he says with a smirk. "I've got this."

I pout, looking back into the living room where our friends have all gathered.

Logan Tate walks around the room, passing out

beers. Lucien and Camille are comfortable in the window seat, chatting with Coach Wilder about their plans to have another kid. Reeves and Saint are arguing about something ridiculous, based on the way Saint is gesticulating and Reeves is shaking his head in pure dismay. Even Eden and Holt are here, exchanging soft whispers by the staircase. Newlyweds are like that.

It's been a little over a year since Alex and I officially got together. For our one-year anniversary, he surprised me with the keys to a small cabin in Ottawa, just north of Saint's cabin. Once we got it decorated the way we liked it, the first order of business was to hold a housewarming party. But when word got around, the housewarming party became a housewarming *weekend* . . . so now our little cabin is brimming with company, most of whom are burly Boston Titans.

"Thank God Saint offered to take a few folks to his place at the end of the night," I say under my breath, shooting Alex a look. He knows how much of an introvert I am, and he's already apologized tenfold for how far the guest list got away from him. "Are you sure I can't—"

"Why don't you go chat with Camille? You were saying that you wanted to get to know her better, weren't you?"

I narrow my eyes at Alex. Something's fishy. He's been busy entertaining guests the whole day, so we've hardly had any time to talk, one-on-one. I guess I won't distract him from making his dinner magic. "All right, fine."

I spend the next hour trying to socialize with the group, but it's hard to keep up with the conversations ping-ponging around me from all sides.

When Alex rings the dinner bell, I'm more than relieved for the change of scenery. We all crowd around the folding tables in the dining room, complimenting Alex on the spread of roasted chicken, casseroles, vegetable medleys, and heaps upon heaps of mashed potatoes. It's a tight squeeze, but we all manage to fit with minimal elbowing.

"Thanks for bringing an extra table and chairs," I say to Saint, who settles in across from me, instantly reaching for a juicy chicken leg.

"Mi casa es tu casa, Scaredy Sprout." He grins at me, and though I haven't heard that nickname in ages, I still roll my eyes.

Dinner is delicious, and everyone is singing Alex's praises by the end of it. I don't think I've ever seen the man flustered, but for a guy who spent an entire season being the villain in everyone else's story, I think he's handling the compliments well.

I catch him staring at me during dessert, but when I smile back, he quickly averts his eyes and resumes his conversation with Coach Wilder.

Weird.

Later, when we're all done eating, I offer to help Alex clear the table and load the dishwasher. He outright refuses my help, gently guiding me back into the living room where the group has gathered for a nightcap.

If Alex wants his space, he can have it. But this doesn't feel like just a space thing. This feels like something else, and a small knot of worry forms inside my stomach.

When I catch Alex dodging me through another doorway, I've finally had enough. I snag his wrist with a firm grip and pull him out onto the deck, where no one can see us. The night breeze ruffles our hair, and I'd comment on how fragrant the fall air is if I weren't dead set on getting Alex to spill whatever's going on with him.

"Are you avoiding me?"

"No. I'm—"

"Seems like you're avoiding me. What are you hiding?"

Alex chuckles, swearing under his breath. "You

really see right through me, don't you?"

I nod, giving him a look that says, *duh*.

"Okay, okay." He lifts his hands in surrender. "I have shitty self-control, right? You know this. I'm losing my mind—fuck, how do I . . ."

I wait patiently with my arms crossed over my chest while he recalibrates. It only takes him a second to get over whatever inner battle he's having with himself, locking his blue eyes on mine.

"Now's as good a time as any. I was planning on doing this tomorrow when everyone left so we'd have more privacy, but . . ."

From his back pocket, Alex pulls out a small black velvet box. Then he sinks to one knee, the stars behind him hanging like a heavenly tapestry.

"Aspen Ford, you have completely turned my life around. Not by trying to change me, just by being your gorgeous self. I think back on the man I was before I met you, and I feel bad for him. Because he didn't know what happiness was yet." His voice catches with emotion. "And now I'm greedy, and I want you in my life for good. I want you to be my wife. I want you to be mine forever. Will you marry me?"

At first I stare at him, a small smile on my lips,

waiting for the punch line. When it doesn't come, the proposal hanging between us finally hits me.

Gripping the front of his sweater, I pull Alex up for a molten kiss. His body presses against mine, his arms wrapping around my waist as he stands, lifting me into the air. I cling to his shoulders, kissing him with all the pent-up emotion I've been carrying around with me this entire day. His hot tongue breaches my lips, meeting mine in a delicious press of wet warmth.

All I can think about is how I could have this man—this *incredible* man—and his fiery kisses for the rest of my life. When we part, I take a gasping breath.

His voice is hoarse when he asks, "So, I'll take that as a yes?"

I laugh through the tears. "Yes!"

He catches my lips again, swallowing my whimper of pure excitement. Because Alex Braun wants me to be his *wife*.

When he lowers my feet back to the deck, our mouths are still melded together in a hopeless tangle. His kisses turn soft and gentle as his thumbs wipe the tears from my cheeks.

"Why did you want to wait until tomorrow?"

"Well, assuming you would say yes, I thought you might like some alone time." He growls, nipping my lower lip with his teeth. "I know I do."

I sigh a little helplessly. "Hmm. How about we sneak off to the lake later, when they all go to sleep? I can wear that swimsuit you like."

He hums his approval. "I like the way you think."

Alex gives me one last lingering kiss before we head back inside. We settle onto the couch together, rejoining the group. Coach Wilder's getting a fire going in the hearth. Saint is in the middle of a story about his latest misadventures in Italy.

Alex and I exchange a secretive look. We can wait to tell our friends about the engagement. There will be plenty of time tomorrow over breakfast.

Until then, it'll be our little secret.

• • •

I hope you enjoyed reading *The Rival*! Up next is Logan Tate and Summer Campbell's story in *The Rookie*. This story holds a BIG piece of my heart. I can't wait for you to find out why. Check out a little sneak preview on the next page.

What to Read Next

the ROOKIE

He has everything a man could want. A lucrative hockey contract. Adoring fans. A family who loves him.

But he's about to throw it all away. Logan Tate's name is dominating the headlines for all the wrong reasons. Instead of goals and assists, the talented young defense man has been racking up fights and suspensions.

I work with athletes who are struggling, but Logan's different. He's not just going to blow his season, but his entire career. And now he can't return to the ice until he deals with his issues, but the stubborn man won't let anyone get close enough to help.

Which is why I packed up and followed him to his family's property in the remote mountains of Colorado. He can't avoid me here.

The only problem?

I can't avoid him either. He's chopping wood and building fires, rescuing my car from snowy ditches, and inviting me to Sunday dinners with his loud extended family. He's a whole lot of man, but beneath all those hard edges is an unexpected tenderness.

Tempted or not, I have to stay out of his bed and get him back to the ice . . . no matter how difficult that might be.

Acknowledgments

Thank you so very much to all the wonderful readers who picked up a copy of *The Rival*. When I started writing book one in this series, *The Rebel*, I didn't think it was possible to love a hero more than I loved Holt Rossi. But then Alex came along and surprised the heck out of me. His redemption arc was irresistible, and I fell for his and Aspen's story hard and fast. As I've wrapped up this story and moved on to Logan Tate's . . . *big happy sigh* . . . let's just say this series keeps getting better and better.

I would also like to extend a big bear hug to my editing team of Pam Berehulke, Rachel Brookes, and Elaine York. You helped me massage my words into something so much better.

Thank you a million billion to the best assistant-slash-business manager an author could ever hope for, Alyssa Garcia. Your support and enthusiasm and gentle guidance are oh so appreciated.

Get Two Free Books

Sign up for my newsletter and I'll automatically send you two free books.

www.kendallryanbooks.com/newsletter

Follow Kendall

Website

www.kendallryanbooks.com

Facebook

www.facebook.com/kendallryanbooks

Twitter

www.twitter.com/kendallryan1

Instagram

www.instagram.com/kendallryan1

Newsletter

www.kendallryanbooks.com/newsletter/

Other Books by Kendall Ryan

Unravel Me

Filthy Beautiful Lies Series

The Room Mate

The Play Mate

The House Mate

Screwed

The Fix Up

Dirty Little Secret

xo, Zach

Baby Daddy

Tempting Little Tease

Bro Code

Love Machine

Flirting with Forever

Dear Jane

Only for Tonight

Boyfriend for Hire

The Two-Week Arrangement

Seven Nights of Sin

Playing for Keeps

All the Way

Trying to Score

Crossing the Line

The Bedroom Experiment

Down and Dirty
Crossing the Line
Wild for You
Taking His Shot
How to Date a Younger Man
Penthouse Prince
The Boyfriend Effect
My Brother's Roommate
The Stud Next Door
The Rebel

For a complete list of Kendall's books, visit:
www.kendallryanbooks.com/all-books/

Printed in Great Britain
by Amazon